Christopher Harvey

Complete Poems Christopher Harvey

being a supplementary volume to the complete works in verse and...

Christopher Harvey

Complete Poems Christopher Harvey
being a supplementary volume to the complete works in verse and...

ISBN/EAN: 9783744772754

Printed in Europe, USA, Canada, Australia, Japan

Cover: Foto ©Andreas Hilbeck / pixelio.de

More available books at **www.hansebooks.com**

The Fuller Worthies' Library.

THE

COMPLETE POEMS OF CHRISTOPHER HARVEY,

M.A.

LONDON :

ROBSON AND SONS, PRINTERS, PANCRAS ROAD, N.W.

The Fuller Worthies' Library.

THE COMPLETE POEMS

OF

CHRISTOPHER HARVEY,

M.A.

FOR THE FIRST TIME FULLY COLLECTED AND COLLATED WITH
THE ORIGINAL AND EARLY EDITIONS; AND IN QUARTO,
WITH ORIGINAL ILLUSTRATIONS.

BEING A

SUPPLEMENTARY VOLUME TO THE COMPLETE WORKS

IN VERSE AND PROSE

OF

GEORGE HERBERT.

Edited by the

REV. ALEXANDER B. GROSART,

ST. GEORGE'S, BLACKBURN, LANCASHIRE.

PRINTED FOR PRIVATE CIRCULATION.
1874.

TO

THE REV. RICHARD WILTON, M.A.

LONDESBOROUGH RECTORY, MARKET WEIGHTON :

DEAR TO ME AS THE POET OF 'WOOD NOTES AND CHURCH BELLS ;'
DEARER AS A FRIEND AND FELLOW-WORKER IN REVIVING
CRASHAW AND HERBERT,
BY CONJOINTLY MAKING THEIR LATIN AND GREEK
'SPEAK ENGLISH' FOR THE FIRST TIME ;
DEAREST OF ALL AS A 'BROTHER BELOVED'
IN SERVING THE ONE MASTER :

I dedicate

THIS COLLECTION OF THE POEMS OF A 'SWEET SINGER,' NOT UNWORTHY
OF THE LOWLY ASSOCIATION WITH GEORGE HERBERT WHICH HE
CLAIMED ; GRATEFUL TO KNOW THAT I MAY WRITE
'AUCTOR PRETIOSA FACIT.'

VERY FAITHFULLY,

ALEXANDER B. GROSART.

CONTENTS.

*** *For readier reference, these Contents are also arranged alphabetically. The figures 1, 2, &c. onward, denote the number of the Poem.*

ILLUSTRATIONS IN 4to.

1. The Grammar School, Kington, Herefordshire: anastatic etching by Rev. W. F. Francis, Great Saxham, Suffolk, after a photograph by Stephens, Kington . . . *facing title-page*

If I am rightly informed, this School has never before been given in any book. As stated in the text (pp. xix.-xx.), it retains still its original quaint and now hoary characteristics. By the kindness of the Rev. C. J. Robinson, M.A., Norton Canon, Weobley—who has done so much to illustrate and elucidate Herefordshire history—I am enabled to furnish the following details concerning this fine old school. It was designed and contracted for in 1622 by John Abel—he finding all materials—for 240*l.*, equal perhaps now to well-nigh 1000*l.* This John Abel was especially skilful in the construction of the timber mansions, ' black and white,' which once were the ornaments of Herefordshire. His chief works were the Town Hall or Market House at Hereford, 1618-20 (long since pulled down) ; Market House at Leominster, 1633 (still standing, but—American fashion—on a different site) ; Market Houses at Brecon, Kington, Weobley ; new church at Abbey Dore; and the present School. He was of great service to the besieged of Hereford in 1645, in constructing defences and mills to grind their corn. On this account he was made by Charles I. one of his Majesty's carpenters. He died in 1694, in the 97th year of his age. His epitaph—composed by himself, and still to be seen on the tomb which he erected for himself in Sarnesfield churchyard—may interest :

' This craggy Stone a covering is for an Architector's Bed,
That lofty Buildings raisèd high, yet now lays low his Head.
His Line and Rule, so Death concludes, are lockèd up in Store ;
Build they who list or they who wist, for he can build no more :
His house of Clay could hold no longer ;
May Heaven's Joy build Him a stronger.

JOHN ABEL.

Vibe ut bibas in bitum æternum.'

Sir John Hawkins, Knight, the illustrious ' navigator' and discoverer, treasurer of the Navy to Queen Elizabeth, was buried in St. Dunstan's in the East, London ; died 12th Nov. 1595. His wife was Margaret Vaughan, Lady of the Bedchamber to Queen Elizabeth; daughter of Charles Vaughan of Hargest (by his wife Margaret, daughter of Sir William Vaughan of Talgark) ; died 2d Feb. 1620. It was by Lady Hawkins's will the Grammar School of Kington was built. I have the greater pleasure in furnishing this Rembrandt-like etching of the ancient Grammar School, in that Wood's blunders in making ' *Thomas Harvey*,' instead of our Christopher Harvey, its first master, and author of ' The Synagogue,' have hitherto dissociated our Worthy from it, and robbed him of his renown as the 'imitator' of 'divine Herbert' (see our Memorial-Introduction, pp. xxi.-ii.).

II. Kington Church: anastatic etching by Rev. W. F. Francis, after photograph by R. Jones, Leominster . *to face page* xvii

III. Clifton on Dunsmore Church: after a photograph . . *Ibid.*

> It shows no 'spire,' agreeably to Dugdale's account as quoted in Memorial-Introduction, p. xx. In connection with a sculptured muzzled bear on the west side of this church there is a singular tradition about it, which is still quick, to wit, that on one occasion the parishioners of Clifton sold their church Bible to buy a bear to bait. Unfortunately for the myth, the sculpture belongs to the fifteenth century, when Bibles were not used in English churches. The bear is in reality the crest of an old family formerly residing at Clifton, viz. a bear sable holding up the dexter paw, the name of the family being *Bereford*, Barford, or Barfoot. In the year 1648 a John Barford appears as one of the eight freeholders who entered into an agreement with the then Lord of the Manor of Clifton, Sir Richard Lucy, for the enclosure of the open and common lands there, and to this John Barford were allotted 96¾ acres of land in lieu of two yards land and a half and two cottage commons. The last of the Barford family at Clifton was married to a Francis about the middle of the last century ; and in 1748 Mr. Robert Francis made a present of the communion-plate—a flagon, chalice, and paten—to Clifton Church. These are engraved with the arms of the Barford family and the crest, *a bear passant*. The daughter of this marriage married a Mr. Bristow, and their daughter a Mr. Jennaway. The allotment of land to John Barford in 1648 was offered for sale by the devisees in trust, under the will of the late Mr. Bethuel Grimes Jenaway, in 1870. The ancient mansion of the Barford family was demolished a few years ago. A story is told of a young man of dissipated habits fond of frequenting two public-houses near the church—the Lion and the Bull—who was accosted on one occasion by a friendly adviser in the following words :
>
> > 'Take heed of the Bull, of the Lion beware ;
> > If you wish to be happy, turn in at the Bear.'
> > (Letter of M. H. Bloxam, Esq., Rugby.)

IV. Autograph of Christopher Harvey, from the parish register of Clifton on Dunsmore—facsimiled by Miss Newall . . *Ibid.*

* These anastatic etchings are from the press of Mr. Stephen H. Cowell, Ipswich. Whitney Church was carried away by the Wye in 1785-6, and was rebuilt in 1740. The present fabric is thus excluded from these Illustrations.

PREFACE.

FROM 1640 onward to the present decade, ' The Synagogue' of CHRISTOPHER HARVEY has accompanied nearly
every edition of ' The Temple' of GEORGE HERBERT, and
I was readily persuaded by many spontaneous Correspondents not to sever the venerable association. I have
deemed it well, nevertheless, to make the Poems of this
Worthy an independent and separate, though companion,
volume to the set of Herbert's Works. Nor was there a
moment's hesitation as to adding ' Schola Cordis' to ' The
Synagogue.' Throughout, ' Schola Cordis' bears the same
mint-mark, and is informed with the same lowly, tender,
sweet spirit as the better known ' Synagogue.' Perhaps
my words toward the close of the Memorial-Introduction
will lead some to '*prove*' that, besides their piety and innocent quaintness, the Poems of Christopher Harvey have
qualities that make them worthy of their long association
with Herbert. It is possible an unsympathetic reader
may feel disposed to liken the placing of ' The Synagogue'
and ' Schola Cordis' beside the marble-work of ' The
Temple,' to those huts one meets with in classic lands
squatting at the foot of once splendid and consecrate
temples. I rather like to think of their association as
symbolised by the swallows' nests hung in metope or
frieze, to their passing stain, perchance, yet by '*imme-
morial lease of love*,' and the glance of swift and burnished

wing and breast, and the tropic note, vindicating their intrusion—if intrusion it be.

'The Synagogue,' as above, was first published in 1640, and then only contained the following :

The Dedication.
Subterliminare—A Stepping-Stone, &c.
The Church-yard.
The Church-stile.
The Church-gate.
The Church-walls.
The Church.
The Church-porch.
Invitation.
Comfort in Extremity.
Resolution and Assurance (divided into three stanzas).
The Nativity.
Vows broken and rewarded [sic, but clearly an error for 'renewed'].
Confusion.
A Paradox.
Inmates.
The Curb [4 st.].
The Loss.
The Search.
The Return [7 st.].
The Circumcision.
Inundations.
Sin [5 st.].
Travels at Home.

It will thus be seen that in the after-editions there was a very considerable increase in the number of pieces. I. L. addressed his ingenious friend, the author of ' The Synagogue,' upon his *additional Church-utensils*. As stated in the relative note, our text is that of the fourth edition, 1661, as the last that could have come under the author's

own eyes. A return thereto has corrected various errors
and restored the genuine orthography. The ninth edition
was published in 1709, along with the thirteenth edition
of ' The Temple.'

' Schola Cordis' was first published in 1647—title-page
on p. 101. By the liberality of HENRY HUTH, Esq., I have
been enabled to reproduce its text. For full details on
this second volume of Harvey's Verse, the reader is re-
ferred to our Memorial-Introduction.

I have now to thank very cordially the following friends
and correspondents for services rendered in my work on
this Worthy: Dr. BRINSLEY NICHOLSON, as before ; W.
ALDIS WRIGHT, Esq., M.A., Trinity College, Cambridge ;
the Rev. WILLIAM LOWE, Bunbury, Cheshire ; Haber-
dashers' Hall, London, through THOMAS WILSON, Esq.,
Harpenden, St. Albans ; the Rev. SAMUEL NEWALL, M.A.,
Clifton on Dunsmore ; the Rev. HENRY DEW, M.A.,
Whitney ; the Rev. JAMES DAVIES, M.A., Moor Court,
Kington ; M. H. BLOXAM, Esq., Rugby.

The Memorial-Introduction will be found to supply
a missing page or two of biography, and the Notes and
Illustrations to elucidate things left obscure. The Glossarial Index will reveal the common use of words and
turns of phrase of 'The Synagogue' and ' Schola Cordis.'
The anastatic etchings of scenes related to Harvey (fur-
nished in the 4to) I owe to the continued interest and
well-trained hands of the Rev. W. FRANCIS FRANCIS,
Great Saxham, Bury St. Edmunds. With reference to
the prose books by Christopher Harvey, described in the
Memorial-Introduction (pp. xxviii.-ix.), I should willingly
give five guineas for them, assured as I am that they will
reveal much of his intellect and heart.

ALEXANDER B. GROSART.

Park View, Blackburn, Lancashire,
June 18, 1874.

MEMORIAL-INTRODUCTION.

CHRISTOPHER HARVEY (or HARVIE[1]), whose Poems it is my privilege (as with so many of these Worthies) for the first time to bring together, has himself very much to blame that so little has come down to posterity concerning him, and that hitherto he has been confounded with another Harvey, and robbed variously of the honour of contributions to the sacred poetry of England notable in their own humble way. For in a gracious little epistle-dedicatory to Sir Robert Whitney of one of the posthumous expositions (viz. of Psalm lxxxv., 1647) of good Thomas Pierson of Brampton-Brian, he avows that 'long agoe' he had 'put on almost an obstinate resolution never to send' his 'own name to the presse, except it' was 'to bring to light another man's labours.' Hence the anonymous title-pages, epistles, &c., of all he published, with the exception of a treatise hereafter to be noticed. The same epistle contains other references that have enabled me to shed a little more light on the long-dimmed memory than others have done, and to correct mistakes of Anthony a-Wood that have gone on uncorrected, as usual, ever since he made them. The epistle thus opens :

'To the Right Worshipfull my truly noble and thrice most honoured patron, Sir Robert Whitney, Knight.[2]

[1] As onward it will be found his father's name is sometimes spelt Harvey and Harvy and sometimes Harvie; and so with his own.

[2] Born 1592, buried 15th September 1653. His widow survived him. Her will, dated 14th September 1667, was proved 20th November 1668.

b

'It is not unknown unto Him, unto Whose eyes all things are naked and opened, that a strong desire doth possesse me (if it be not more proper to call it ambition) of offering to the present age, and leaving to posterity, some publick evidence of that unfeigned thankfulnesse, which I humbly acknowledge to be due unto you, for your altogether undeserved as well as unexpected at the first, *and now little lesse than twenty years'* continued favour, expressed amongst many other particulars by *three severall presentations unto such Church-livings as were in your power to dispose of;* and those not only so freely, but also so friendly, not granted, but offered, that would be the severest censurer of symonie that ever was chose of purpose a pattern in that particular for patrons perpetually to practise by, the world could not afford him any one that might more truly say than you can, *Nec prece, nec precis.*'

Dated in 1647, the 'little less than *twenty years'* of this epistle takes us back to about 1629, and the '*three severall presentations'* indicated, find partial elucidation at any rate in these Facts : (*a*) In 1629-30 the following entry occurs in the register of Whitney : 'Anne, the daughter of Christopher Harvey and Margaret his wife, was baptized March 13th, 1630.' Another entry informs us that 'William Huddleston, clerck, Rector of Whitney, was buryed December 19th, 1630.' It thus appears that Harvey was living at Whitney before he himself became its rector, which he did upon the death of Huddleston. Probably he was acting as 'assistant' to his predecessor while the old man 'walked' slowly and lingeringly along the valley of the shadow of death. These other 'baptism' entries at Whitney carry us forward to 1639—the first a very remarkable Christian name, but not without suggestiveness in the recollection of Christopher Marlowe's mighty tragedy (1586) of 'Tamburlaine the Greate':

(2) Tamberlane, the sonne of Christopher Harvey, clerck, and Margaret his wife, was baptized July 7, 1633.

(3) John, yᵉ sonne of Christopher Harvey, clerck, and Margaret his wife, baptized June 21, 1635.

(4) Robert, the sonne of Christopher Harvey, clerck, and Margaret his wife, was baptized July 30, 1637.

(5) Hellen, the daughter of Christopher Harvey, clerck, and Margaret his wife, was baptized September 22, 1639.

With the last all notice of Christopher Harvey at Whitney ends.

(*b*) In the original 'Register Booke, or a Perfect Account both of Schoolmasters and Scholars,' &c., of the Grammar School of Kington, Herefordshire, the first entry runs : ' Mem. that the day and yeare in the margin mentioned (A.D. 1632, Septemb. 29), Christopher Harvey, Mʳ of Arts, late rector of the parish church of Whitney . . . was, by direction from Captain Anthony Lewes, Esq., one of the executors of the last will and testament of the said Lady [=Dame Margaret Hawkins, widow of the circumnavigator ; her maiden name Vaughan], admitted by us the first prælector or head schoolmaster of the said school :

John Vaughan.

James Vaughan,' &c.

The word '*late* Rector of Whitney' would seem to show that Harvey had resigned that 'living' in 1632 for the schoolmastership of Kington. His patron-friend Whitney was one of the School's trustees. Perhaps the baptism-entries on to 1639 point to a mild kind of 'symonie,' as noted in the epistle *supra*. Or is the explanation that Harvey resigned Whitney conditionally? He must have continued master at Kington a very short time, being appointed Sept. 29, 1632, while David Meredith was made his successor March 25, 1633. So he seems to have quietly returned to Whitney, as the baptism-entries imply. The importance of this newly-found bit of fact will appear immediately. Meantime, possessors of our quarto will be gratified with a cunningly-rendered anastatic etching of the venerable school, with the hoar of centuries on it now and a

piquant quaintness of look.[1]   (c) On 14th November
1639, Christopher Harvey was instituted to the vicarage
of Clifton-on-Dunsmore, Warwickshire, on the presentation of Sir Robert Whitney of Whitney. His 'presentation' was coincident with a fact given by Dugdale
in his county history of Warwickshire, as follows under
Clifton : 'Here was a fair spire steeple, as an eminent
landmark, seen over all the part of the countrey in regard of its height and situation of the place ; which in
the year 1639 was pull'd down to save the costs of its
repair' (p. 9, edition 1765, folio). The following baptism
entries are from the parish register of Clifton on Dunsmore :

(1) Bridgett and Mary, [twin] daughters of Christopher Harvey and Margaret his wife, were baptized June
12, 1642.

(2) Witney, the son of Christopher Harvey and Margaret his wife, was baptized September 24, 1643 ; and,
alas, 'buryed' October 11th, 1643 ; thus

'No sooner borne then blasted.'

(3) Thomas, the son of Christopher Harvey and Margaret his wife, was baptized February 22, 1645.

Turning back on these 'three severall presentations,'
there can be no doubt that they answer throughout to the
words of the epistle-dedicatory to the gallant Cavalier Sir
Robert Whitney ; while another epistle (to exposition by
Pierson of Psalm lxxxvii.), 'to the right vertuous and
religious, my most honoured ladie, the Ladie Anne Whitney,' similarly acknowledges obligation to this famous
daughter of Sir Thomas Lucy of Charlecote.[2]   It will be

[1] See note on page xi. ante, for information on this school.
[2] I have concluded that Kington School was one of the three
'preferments' to which Harvey alludes, because, though Sir Robert
Whitney was not the actual patron, his influence was absolute from
his family position and relationship to the Vaughans. It is just

observed, too, that the little son 'Witney' (or Whitney) drew his brief-worn name from his father's friends. But the mastership of Kington Grammar School is most of all to be remembered, seeing that Anthony a-Wood designated *Thomas* Harvey as 'the first master of Kington School,' and, what is worse, 'the author of "The Synagogue," in imitation of divine Herbert.' With an uncharacteristic lack of inquisitiveness, Wood, in chronicling, sub George Turbervile ('Athenæ,' i. 628, ed. Bliss), translations of Eclogues of Mantuan, remarks: 'The said eclogues were afterwards translated by another hand; but not without the help of that translation of Turbervile, though not acknowledged. The person that performed it was Thomas Harvey, who writes himself gent. But whether the same Thomas Harvey who was master of arts, the first master of Kington School in Herefordshire (founded 1620), and the author of "The Synagogue," in imitation of divine Herbert, *I know not.*' It is a pity he did not exercise his usual painstaking, when he would have discovered that Christopher, not Thomas, was 'the first master of Kington School,' and Christopher, not Thomas, Harvey author of 'The Synagogue.' The 'Thomas Harvey, *gent*,' was a translator, with some salt of wit, of various Italian and Latin poets, as 'The Bucolicks of Baptist Mantuan, in Ten Eclogues. Translated out of Latine into English, by Tho. Harvey, Gent' (1656), and 'The Latine Epigrams of John Owen, late one of the Fellows of New Colledge in Oxford. Rendred into English by Thomas Harvey, Gent. Once a Commoner in the Colledge at Winchester' (1677). In the 'Fasti' (ii. 9) there is a notice of 'William Harvey, son of Thomas Harvey, gent, by Joan Halke his wife; born at Folkstone in Kent on the second day of April 1578.' Query, the 'Thomas

---

possible that the associated chapel-of-ease with Clifton may have been the third. The Rector of Clifton then drew its revenues.

Harvey, Gent,' *supra?* or was this the great discoverer
of the circulation of the blood, renowned Dr. William
Harvey? So elsewhere. The invariable occurrence of his
name in full to all he published, and the as invariable
addition of 'Gent' (that is, gentleman), enable us to set
aside in another way Wood's mistake, and also a similar
one—of which more in the sequel—on 'Schola Cordis.'
Izaak Walton here furnishes undoubtable testimony. In
the 'Complete Angler' he quotes a poem from 'The
Synagogue' (viz. 13. The Book of Common Prayer, pp.
17-18), and puts in margin to it the name of 'Christopher
Harvie;' and that he knew the man is shown by these
three things : (1) That he himself wrote a commendatory
poem *to his friend* the author of 'The Synagogue' (see it
onward). (2) That in the 'Complete Angler' he calls him
'a friend of mine.' (3) That Christopher Harvey in turn
addressed a commendatory poem on the 'Complete Angler,' given onward. Further, Walton calls him in the
prefix to the poem before 'The Synagogue' 'my reverend
friend,' and in the 'Complete Angler' in making the quo-
tation 'a divine.' Now Thomas Harvey was not 'master
of Kington School,' and not 'reverend' or 'a divine,' but
ostentatiously ' *Gent.*'

It will summarise the matter to give here successively
—(*a*) the heading of Walton's poem ; (*b*) Walton's words
in 'Complete Angler ;' (*c*) Harvey's poem to Walton.

(*a*) *Heading of Walton's poem to Harvey.*
To my Reverend Friend the Author of 'The Synagogue.'

(*b*) *Walton's words in ' Complete Angler,'* chap. v.

' *Ven.* I thank you, good master, for your good direction for fly-fishing, and for the sweet enjoyment of the
pleasant day, which is, so far, spent without offence to
God or man. And I thank you for the sweet close of
your discourse with Mr. Herbert's verses, who, I have

heard, loved angling; and I do the rather believe it, because he had a spirit suitable to anglers, and to those primitive Christians that you love and have so much commended.

' *Pisc.* Well, my loving scholar, and I am pleased to know that you are so well pleased with my direction and discourse. And since you like these verses of Mr. Herbert's so well, let me tell you what a *reverend and learned divine* [in margin, *Ch. Harvie*] that professes to imitate him, and has indeed done so most excellently, hath writ of our Book of Common Prayer, which I know you will like the better, because he is *a friend of mine*, and I am sure no enemy to angling.

" What! Pray'r by th' book? and common? Yes; why not?" '

(c) *Christopher Harvey's poem to Walton, prefixed to second edition of the ' Complete Angler' (1655).*

To the Reader of the Complete Angler.
First, mark the title well; my friend that gave it
Has made it good; this book deserves to have it:
For he that views it with judicious looks
Shall find it full of art, baits, lines, and hooks.
The world the river is; both you and I
And all mankind are either fish or fry;
If we pretend to reason, first or last
His baits will tempt us, and his hooks hold fast.
Pleasure or profit, either prose or rhime,
If not at first will doubtlesse take's in time.
Here sits in secret blest Theologie,
Waited upon by grave Philosophie
Both naturall and morall; Historie
Deck'd and adorn'd with flowers of poetrie,
The matter and expression striving which
Shall most excel in worth, yet not seem rich:
There is no danger in his baits; that hook
Will the safest that is surest took.
Nor are we caught alone, but (which is best)
We shall be wholsom and be toothsom drest:
Drest to be fed, not to be fed upon ;
And danger of a surfet here is none.

The solid food of serious contemplation
Is sauc'd here with such harmlesse recreation,
That an ingenuous and religious minde
Cannot inquire for more than it may finde
Ready at once prepar'd, either t' excite
Or satisfie a curious appetite.
    More praise is due ; for 'tis both positive
And truth, which once was interrogative,
And utter'd by the poet then in jest,
    Et piscatorem piscis amare potest.

C. H., Master of Arts.

It may be safely assumed, with all this concurrent evidence, that Anthony a-Wood, misinformed as to Thomas
Harvey having been 'the first master of Kington School,'
was also misinformed on the authorship of 'The Synagogue,' much as he was in assigning the well-known Poems
of Southwell to John Davies of Hereford.

Another line of research has yielded us additional
Facts, that go to give definiteness to an indefinite statement of Wood, and to explain how it came to pass that
our Worthy is found in Herefordshire, viz. at Whitney and
Kington.

First of all, in preparing our Memoir of learned and
saintly SAMUEL TORSHELL—for the reprint in Nichol's
Puritan Commentaries of Stock and Torshell on Malachi
(1865)—I discovered that a Christopher Harvey was the
'preacher' at Bunbury, Cheshire, in association with 'holy'
William Hinde, the golden-penned biographer of John
Bruen of Bruen-Stopford. This Christopher Harvey I find
from the ancient Records of the Haberdashers' Company
of London, in whom vests the 'presentation' to Bunbury,
must have been among the first, if not the very first,
preacher and schoolmaster (both apparently united in one)
of the place, founded by moneys and lands 'delivered' and
'conveyed' to the 'master and wardens' by one of their
own members, 'Mr. Thomas Aldersey,' as appears by these
extracts :

(1) 1594. 'Mr. T. Aldersey delivered to the Mr. [master] and wardens the some of £300, to the use of the company for ever, to be employed in purchasing of land or otherwise, as to the Mr., wardens, and assistants of the worshipful company for the tyme being, or the more part of them, shall seem good in their discretion, they giving yearly for ever £viii. to eight poor householders of the company, according to former order taken in that behaulf; the same to be yearly distributed thereto forever, by his appointment, on the morrow of the elecson of the master and wardens of this worshipful company, and the first payment to be on the morrow after the next elecson daie now next comynge ; and it is ordered that the master and wardens shall set the seale of the house for the sealing of such counterparts of wryting and other things as is needful to be done about Mr. Aldersey's busyness, touchinge the tythes of Bunbery and other lands that are to be conveyed to the use of the free schoole there ; and this is to be their warrant on that behaulf.'

(2) 2d November 1597. 'At the request of Mr. John Aldersey, and for the better despatch of the business of Mr. Aldersey's schoole and other things touching that corporacion in Cheshire, it is ordered that a letter of attorney shalbe made from the governors of the said school to one John Aldersey of Spurstowe, in the county of Chester, gentleman, to collect the rents and revenues of the land assured to that corporacion by Mr. John Aldersey, wherein it is thought convenyent that there shalbe conteyned a covenant on the behaulf of the said John Aldersey, that he shall well and trulie paie and destribute out of his receipts such somes of money to the preacher, the schoolemaster, and others in the parish of Boneburie, as is thereto paid and distributed according to the order sett downe and provided in that behaulf ; and that he shall accompt yearly for the same and the residue of his receipts, with proviso that the same letter of attourney shall not stand

any longer in force than it shall seem good to the governors aforesaid.'

Then specifically:

(3) 14th July 1600. ' First [=the first business before
the Court that day], on reading of a letter sent to our
master and wardens from Mr. Christopher Harvie, Mr.
Aldersey's preacher at Bunbury in Cheshire, containing
the names of the schollers and the order of their proceed-
ing and the state of the school there, it is ordered that a
letter shalbe sent unto him from our master and wardens
in answer thereof, desyringe him to persevere and continue his care unto the schoole, as he hath already done
according to the trust reposed in him.'

These extracts are all of distinct statement remaining
in the old records—searched diligently backward to 1590—
and they leave the date of the first preachership and the
date of the appointment of Christopher Harvey undeter-
minable. But it seems clear that in 1600 he was the
preacher, and probably was at once given the post by Mr.
Aldersey in 1594-5. I fix on 1594-5, because the letters
patent of Queen Elizabeth are dated 2d January 1594 ;
the lease A.D. 1595; and Thomas Aldersey's own will 20th
February 1595. Then in the statutes ' prescribed, limited,
and ordained by Thomas Aldersey, citizen and haber-
dasher,' Article 12 reads: ' Item : the preacher for the
time being shall have and enjoy for his dwelling-house
that messuage or tenement with the appurtenances and all
the lands which he, the said Thomas Aldersey, purchased
of Thomas Bonebury, Esq., all which he now uses, *and
occupied by Christopher Harvey the preacher*, their or his
assignes.' This must have been before 1595. Unfortu-
nately the registers of the church—a very fine miniature-
cathedral one—of Bunbury are fragmentary, and do not
include 1597. Among the earliest entries is the burial of
the good preacher :

1601, 23 N[ovember], Xtopher Harvy, preachr of Bunb.

But though we are thus deprived of the satisfaction of finding the 'baptism' of our Christopher Harvey in the register, it will be immediately seen that he was certainly son of the preacher of Bunbury. Wood describes him as ' a minister's son of Cheshire,' and that he was 'aged sixteen years' in 1613, which gives his birth as 1597, or exactly in agreement with the preceding data.[1]

A further entry in the Bunbury register makes the identity still more certain, viz. the following:

Matrimonia, 1608 [=1609 according to our style].

Feb. 21. Thomas Pierson of Waverham, presbyter, and Ellen Harvie of Bunburie, Wid[ow].

This 'Thomas Pierson' of Waverham was the afterwards celebrated Thomas Pierson of Brampton-Brian, the editor of the Works of William Perkins, the chosen friend of the Harleys, and the 'savoury' expositor of certain of the Psalms. Here is explained our Christopher Harvey's migration to Herefordshire and his loving publication of Pierson's expositions. His mother in her widowhood having become Pierson's wife, Master Christopher, born in 1597, would be in his twelfth year at the date of the marriage. His stepfather Pierson loved him as his own child— all the more, perchance, that he had none of his own—and the epistles-dedicatory to the posthumously published expositions show that Harvey reciprocated the affection, not to say that he reverenced him with pathetic wistfulness. It is extremely satisfying to have been enabled thus by widely-gleaned memoranda to recover the personality of the 'sweet singer' of 'The Synagogue.'[2] No

[1] One separate sheet at Bunbury contains the baptism-entries to 1578. There is then a gap, and the regular entries are not resumed until 1598.

[2] The following entries at Bunbury are placed here as they probably belong to the same family of Harveys:

Sepulturæ.

1619. May 20. John, the son of James Harvy of Bunbury.

doubt our Worthy was first of all educated in the Grammar School of Bunbury, with his venerable father's eye
on him. The 'Athenæ' and 'Fasti' furnish these further
Facts : that Christopher Harvey 'became a batler [=poor
scholar : and be it remembered, Jeremy Taylor was entered *pauper scholaris*] of Brasen-nose Coll. in 1613, aged
[as *supra*] 16 years ; took the degrees in arts [Bachelor
of Arts, May 10, 1617 ; 'Fasti,' i. 369], that of master being
compleated 1620 [May 10 ; ' Fasti,' i. 393]; holy orders ; and
at length was made Vicar of Clifton [with Dunsmore] in
Warwickshire.' Wood also records the following work
by him : 'The Right Rebel. A Treatise discovering the
true Use of the Name by the Nature of Rebellion, with

Baptismata.

1620. June 11. Mary, the daughter of James Harvy of Wood-
ward Green.

1627. August 6. John, the son of John Harvey of Tearton
[=Tiverton].

1628. Jan. 18. Elizabeth, the daughter of James Harvey of Cal-
veley.

Matrimonia.

1605. Jan. 28. John Smith and Margaret Harvey.

1618 (N.S. 1619). January 4. James Harvy and Elizabeth Jones,
both of this parish.

1629. Septem. 13. John Williamson of Burwardsley, and Jane
Harvie of Tilston.

It may be permitted me to refer to my full Memoir of Pierson in the
reprint of his Expositions of certain Psalms (1868. Nichol's Puritan
Commentaries), where, for the first time, a noticeable life is ade-
quately treated. With reference to the elder Christopher Harvey of
Bunbury, it is interesting and pleasant to know that an eminent
successor of his—Samuel Torshell—remembered him in his noble
sermon at the funeral of Mr. John Moulson of Hargrave, at Bunbury
('Home of Mourning' (1672), sermon xx.) ; *e.g.* 'He began to sort
himself with the gravest company, chiefly with that learned and
godly Master Christopher Harvey, sometime incumbent in this
church, to whom he was dear.'

the Properties and Practices of Rebels. Applicable to all
both old and new Phanatics. Lond. 1661 (oct.).' . . .
'Faction supplanted: or, a Caveat against the ecclesias-
tical and secular Rebels, in two Parts. 1. A Discourse concerning the Nature, Properties, and Practices of Rebels.
2. Against the Inconstancy and inconsistent Contrariety
of the same Men's Pretensions and Practices, Principles
and Doctrines. Lond. 1663 (oct.); pen'd mostly in 1642,
and finished 3 Ap. 1645.' He remarks of the latter: 'This
book, I suppose (for I have not seen it or the other), is the
same with the former, only a new title put to it, to make
it vend the better.' Further: 'Another book goes under
his name, called "Conditions of Christianity," printed at
Lond. in two; but that, or any other besides, I have not
yet seen.' Wood also notices his publication of Pierson's
Expositions ('Athenæ,' iii. 538). No more than Wood have
I succeeded in finding either of the two books named;
but Pickering's Herbert (1853, vol. ii. p. 291) to the first
title-page prefixes ' ΑΦΗΝΙΑΣΤΗΣ or . . . ,' and gives the
name and publisher and collation in full: 'by *Christopher
Harvey*, Vicar of *Clifton*, in the county of *Warwick*. *Lond.*
Printed for *R. Royston*, Bookseller to his sacred Majesty,
1661 ;' oct. p. 176, besides title, dedication (to Sir Geoffery
Palmer, Knight and Bart.), and preface, eight leaves.

It is vexatious that the 'Right Rebel' and 'Conditions'
should thus have disappeared.

Harvey was fortunate in all his locations (if an Ame-
ricanism be permitted), from his Bethlehem-like birth-
place in antique Bunbury to his pleasant rectory on the
Wye at Whitney and his school at Kington, and finally
in semi-historical Clifton-on-Dunsmore on the rocky
shores of the Avon. These outward facts alone survive
in relation to the last—viz. (*a*) In 1653, under a decree of
the Court of Chancery, he was appointed a trustee of
neighbouring Rugby School by the designation of Christopher Harvey, Esquire, of Clifton, it having been not

then unusual to designate well-born clergymen as 'Esquire,' as witness burial-entry of George Herbert. (*b*) The register under 4th of April 1663 enters, 'buried Mr. Christopher Harvey, Vicar of Clifton.' (*c*) There is no monument to his memory ; but in the churchyard, south of the chancel, and not many feet from it, is a low flat tomb, with a moulding on the verge, of the seventeenth century. This tomb is uninscribed, but is supposed by an antiquary in the neighbourhood to have covered the remains of Christopher Harvey. Within the church of Clifton nothing remains of the early woodwork or church furniture, even the ancient font, in which Thomas Carte the historian —a native of Clifton—was baptised by immersion, being gone ; but externally it is the same as in Harvey's time.[1] I do not doubt, accordingly, that our anastatic etching of it after a photograph (in 4to) will be acceptable. Curiously enough there is a chapel-of-ease to the mother-church of Clifton — Brownsever Chapel — considered by competent authority to have been erected in the eleventh or twelfth century, very similar in size and general appearance to the church of George Herbert at Bemerton.[2]

---

[1] Samuel Carte baptised all his family by immersion. See below for more on successors of Harvey.

[2] The present Incumbent of Clifton-on-Dunsmore (Rev. Samuel Newall, M.A.) has communicated to me various interesting memoranda on three of his predecessors. This is scarcely the place for utilising them in full, but their names and a little more may be recorded here: (*a*) Samuel Carte, Prebendary of Lichfield, was inducted into the vicarage on 27th March 1684. He is still remembered as an accomplished antiquary, but mainly as the father of Thomas Carte the Historian of Ormonde. (*b*) Bartholomew Fox, inducted into the vicarage on 4th September 1733. He claimed to be a descendant of the martyrologist. He was interred 3d April 1780. (*c*) The Rev. J. H. C. Moor, B.D., was curate and vicar from June 1803 to March 1853. A vol. of his 'Sermons' was published in 1855. Pickering's Herbert (1853: vol. ii. p. 291) mistakenly names him Vicar of Rugby. It may be added that Edward Cave, the first

The authorship of 'The Synagogue' having been vindicated for Christopher Harvey as against the blunder of Anthony a-Wood in assigning it to Thomas Harvey, Gent, it is only required that the Facts be told concerning 'Schola Cordis.' Like 'The Synagogue'—as we have seen —'Schola Cordis' was issued anonymously in 1647. A second edition was also published anonymously in 1664, 'for Lodowick Lloyd at the Castle in Cornhill.' A third edition appeared in 1675, and on its title-page after 'Emblems' comes—' by the *Author* of the SYNAGOGUE annexed to Herbert's poems. Whereunto is Added, The Learning of the Heart, by the same Hand. The third edition. London, Printed for Lodowick Lloyd.' 'The Learning of the Heart' was given in the 1647, and I have seen it in copies of that of 1664, though not named in either of their title-pages. It will be observed that the same publisher issued both the second and third editions. All the three engraved titles are different; but the 'Emblems' themselves—of which more anon—are from the same plates.

Mr. W. C. Hazlitt in his 'Bibliography of Old English Literature' commits several errors about 'Schola Cordis.' First of all, he places it under Thomas Harvey, on the allegation that while Sir John Hawkins ascribed the book and 'The Synagogue' to Christopher Harvey, he is opposed by Wood in this assertion. Neither Wood nor Hawkins so much as names 'Schola Cordis.' Moreover if Mr. Hazlitt accepted Wood's imagined assignment of 'Schola Cordis' to Thomas Harvey, why did he not place 'The Synagogue' also under his name? There is not a shadow of proof that Thomas Harvey ever claimed one syllable of 'Schola Cordis.' He put his own name in full to all his books. He was also

---

Sylvanus Urban of the 'Gentleman's Magazine,' and whose life Dr. Johnson wrote, was a native of the township of Newton in Clifton parish, having been born in a house which is still called Cave's Inn. The old Clifton Vicarage is now used as a farmhouse.

still living in 1675, when the third edition was published.
But indeed his non-authorship of 'The Synagogue,' *cœteris
paribus*, involves his non-authorship of 'Schola Cordis.'
Internally no one could for a moment imagine the mere-
tricious translator of 'Mantuan' writing one line of 'Schola Cordis.' Modern reprints of 'Schola Cordis' in 1808,
1812, 1823, and even so recently as 1866, misled by the
word 'Emblems' and a very superficial resemblance in the
opening of the first Emblem to his well-known Emblems,
boldly as ignorantly put the name of Francis Quarles on
the title-page. This odd blunder is one of the 'Curiosities
of Literature' worthy of a place in a revised D'Israeli. It
is only a typical example of how hastily and perfunctorily
much editorial work is done.

'Schola Cordis' derives its engravings—very poor as a
whole—from the Dutch Haeften, with the exception of i.
ii. and iii., engraved by William Marshall. To Haeften
also belong the hexameters and texts from iv. to xlvii.
Whose those of i. to iii. are does not appear ; nor is it of
any moment. The texts of these three, unlike the rest,
are not from the Vulgate. With reference to the Verse—
called Odes and Epigrams—an examination of Haeften
shows that Harvey took from him only the general idea
and the subjects and texts (exclusive of i. to iii.). The
Odes and Epigrams are his own. These details may interest, as showing Haeften's and Harvey's plans and (ap-
parent) reasons for arranging their quotations and texts
as they have done :

Lib. i. This is a kind of introduction to 'The School,'
the 'Emblems' commencing with Lib. ii.

Lib. ii. Aversi Cordis ad Deum conversio et directio.
Prima Classis : Cordis Aversio, Embl. i.-vii.=iv-10, Har-
vey ; Secundi Classis : Cordis Reversio et Expurgato,
Embl. viii.-xiv.=xi.-xvii., Harvey ; Tert. Classis : Cordis
Oblatio et Examen, Embl. xv.-xx=xviii.-xxiii., Harvey.

Lib. iii. Dei erga Cor humanum beneficia. Quarta Classis: Cordis Illuminatio et Spiritualis Profectus, Embl. xxi.-xxxi., *i.e.* Cor renov.—C. dilitatio; Quinta Classis: Cordis perfectio et cum Christo Unio, Embl. xxxii.-xxxix., *i.e.* C. inhab.—C. Quies.

Lib. iv. Exercitatio Cordis in Christi Passione Præfatio. De utilitate medilandi passionem Domini nostri Jesu Christi. Sexta Classis: Peregrinatio Cordis cum Christi Patiente, Embl. xl.-xlvii., *i.e.* Baln. C.—Compunct. C.; Septima Classis: Cordis cum Cruce et Crucifixo Conformatio, Embl. xlviii.-lv., *i.e.* C. in cruce exp.—Thal. C. &c.

I have not put in the Harvey numbers in books iii. iv. because then the arrangement begins to vary, and while i.-xxviii. of Haeften run parallel with iv.-xxxi. of Harvey and in same order, there are subsequently differences; *e.g.* the engraving in Harvey opposite xxxi. is a reduplication by error of xli. Then xxx. Cordis Scalæ is xxxvii. Harvey; xxxi. is xxxv.; xxxii. is xxxiv.; xxxiv. is xxxiii.; xxxv. is xxxvi.; xxxvi. is xxxii.; xxxvii. is xxxviii.; xxxviii. is xxxix.; and so on one in advance in Harvey to xliv.=xlv.; then xlvii. is xlvi.; lii. is xlvii. Harvey omits the following altogether:

xxix. Cordis Protectio: Dedisti eis scutum cordis laborem tuum (Thren. iii. 65).

xxxiii. Obsignatio Cordis: Pone me ut signaculum, super cor tuum (Cant. viii. 6).

xlv. Pictura Cordis ex sindone Veronicæ expressa: Signatum est super nos lumen vultus tui Domine (Psal. iv. 7).

xlvi. Cor Phiala Christo sitienti: Dabo tibi poculum ex vino condito (Cant. viii. 2).

xlviii. Cordis in cruce expansio: In simplicitate cordis quærite illum (Sap. i. 1).

xlix. Crucis in corde Plantatio: Plantatio Domino ad glorificandum (Isaice lxi. 3).

l. Dedicatio Cordis Titulo Crucis: Titulus Domini

c

juxta terminum altaris erit in signum et in testimonium
Domino exercituum (Isaice xix. 19).

li. Apertio Cordis Lanceâ Longini : Vulnerata chari-
tate ego sum (Cant. ii. 5).

liii. Azylum Cordis in latere vulnerato : Esto quasi
columba nidificans in summo ore foraminis (Jerem. xlviii.
28).

liv. Speculum Cordis in quinque vulneribus : Inspice
et fac secundum exemplar quod tibi in monte monstratum
est (Exod. xxv. 40).

lv. Thalamus Cordis in Christi sepulchro : Consepulti
sumus cum Christo (Rom. vi. 4).

The engraved frontispiece (or title-page) of Harvey's
' Schola Cordis' is an exceedingly poor and reversed copy
of Haeften's.   The ' Emblems' in Haeften are far superior
to those in Harvey's book—indeed those in Haeften of
1629 are wonderfully soft.   Those of 1663, though from
the same plates, are so inferior that they must have been
used in intermediate editions and often retouched.   Van
Lochem in Harvey seems to have traced his from the back,
at least xviii.-xxix. and xlvii. are reversed.   The rest are
not reversed, but must have all been traced in the principal
parts and occasionally in a glass ; for though the faces differ,
and there are slight variations in the hair and of the back-
placed foot, yet the general resemblance in the proportions
and attitudes of the figures and the folds of flying scarfs
is too close to be accounted for by mere copying by eye.

One cannot quite understand why Harvey omitted
some that he has omitted, as for instance Haeften's xxxiii.
Obsignato cordis, &c.; but he appears in all the other cases
to have avoided any Emblem with a cross or such repre-
sentations as contained the inscription INRI as l., or the
wounded body of Christ, liii.-iv.   Yet he has illustrated
one of the Emblems showing the ' five wounds.'   It is a
pity he did not take lv. with its Consepulti sumus cum
Christo, together with the rest of the passage, or it and

then the rest of the passage as a final Emblem. He would thereby have had a better close and ending of the whole.

It is characteristic of Harvey's humble self-estimate that in 'The Synagogue' he sought to 'imitate' with distant footstep 'The Temple,' and that in 'Schola Cordis' he accepted the Emblems and texts of Haeften. This modesty of his similarly leads him to adopt even Herbert's oddities of form, as his Easter Wings, which in Harvey is reproduced in Ode xxxviii. (pp. 208-10) and in Ode xxxvii. (pp. 205-7). His notices of himself are likewise shaped on Herbert's of himself, *e.g.* p. 149. So throughout; and yet equally throughout there is evidence of a very distinct individuality, as well as of a singularly holy and consecrate life. The 'tune' of the Poetry may be no more than that of a 'singing brook' under the leaves, yet is it a God-given 'tune,' with melodies and harmonies and changes to the listening and stooped ear.

Turning to 'The Synagogue,' these additional notes of Coleridge—additional to those incorporated in our Notes and Illustrations—on certain of the poems in it are of value :

P. 46, The Nativity, &c. The only poem in 'The Synagogue' which possesses *poetic* merit ; with a few changes and additions this would be a striking poem.

Mr. C[oleridge] proposes to substitute the following for the fifth to the eighth line :

> 'To sheath or blunt one happy ray,
> That wins new splendour from the day.
> This day that gives the power to rise,
> And shine on hearts as well as eyes ;
> This birthday of all souls, when first
> On eyes of flesh and blood did burst
> That primal great lucific light,
> That rays to thee, to us gave sight.'

P. 56, Whitsunday. The spiritual miracle was the descent of the Holy Ghost ; the outward the wind and the tongues ; and so St. Peter himself explains it. That each individual obtained the power of speaking all languages, is neither contained in nor fairly deducible from St. Luke's account.

P. 59, ' All reason doth *transcend*.' Most true ; but not *contradict*. Reason is to faith as the eye to the telescope. (Coleridge's Notes, from Pickering's Herbert, 1835, onward).

P. 10, ' The best and most forcible sense of a word is often that which is contained in its etymology. The author of the poems (" The Synagogue") . . . gives the original purport of the word integrity :

> " Next to sincerity, remember still
> Thou must resolve upon *integrity*.
> God will have *all* thou hast—thy mind, thy will,
> Thy thoughts, thy words, thy works."

And again, after some verses on constancy and humility, the poem concludes with :

> " He that desires to see
> The face of God, in his religion must
> Sincere, *entire*, constant, and humble be,"'

(' The Friend,' vol. i. p. 53, edition 1837.)

I must demur to the *dictum* that The Nativity is the only poem of ' The Synagogue' of ' *poetic* merit' as I must prefer Harvey's own simpler if ruggeder lines to the Coleridge version. The student will find several other complete poems of true ' poetic merit,' and many a line and epithet and quaint conceit such as only a real Maker could have given us. I have always deemed the opening of 17. Communion Plate as demonstrative of an imaginative faculty in *kind* resembling Herbert and Vaughan's. The noblest use of gold is surely very fine. Then his entitling the Book of God as the ' god of books' (p. 21) is very memorable, and has been often since misassigned to others.

The Notes and Illustrations to the poems and the Glossarial Index will guide to a goodly number of somewhat out-of-the-way words and phrases and compound epithets and conceits which are common to 'The Synagogue' and 'Schola Cordis.' The rhythm and entire *mode* of expression are also alike. The student-reader will be abundantly rewarded if he give an hour or two to study the thinking and the feeling of Odes ix. xiv. xvi. xvii. xviii. xix. xxiii. xxv. xxvi. xxviii. and xxx. There are subtleties and daintinesses in all of these—to name no more—that seem to me exquisite.

Altogether this Worthy stands out a very venerable and lovable man and a genuine Singer, as well as of 'the godly best divines' whose 'lives,' as old Samuel Rowlands sang in his 'Fooles Bolt is Soone Shot' (1614),

> ' according to their doctrine shine,
> That have not their religion all in tongue.'

As a Poet his note is true as a singing-bird's, and there is throughout the felt presence of The Master. And so to shy, modest, hiding Christopher Harvey may there be given all kindliest greeting and welcome by a new and enlarged circle of friends! If comparisons with Herbert as a Poet show him far beneath him, let Timothe Kendall's pleading (1577) avail :

> ' Now, reader, lende thy listyning care,
> And after synging larke,
> Content thy self of chattyng crow
> Some homely notes to marke.'
>
> ('Trifles.')

Altogether and intrinsically the gentle Singer of 'The Synagogue' and of ' Schola Cordis' will abundantly reward sympathetic days spent over his lowly pages. Be it remembered that one of his poems, Of the Book of Common-prayer, was in the mind of Elia when he thus wrote to Coleridge, 28th October 1796 : ' Among all your quaint readings, did you ever light upon Walton's " Complete Angler"?   I asked you the question once before ; it breathes the very spirit of innocence, purity, and simplicity of heart; *there are many choice old verses interspersed in it;* it would sweeten a man's temper at any time to read it ; it would christianise every discordant angry passion : pray make yourself acquainted with it.'   Charles Lamb rarely misestimates or exaggerates.

ALEXANDER B. GROSART.

I.

THE SYNAGOGUE;

OR

THE SHADOW OF THE TEMPLE.

NOTE.

Opposite is given the title-page of the last edition of the Synagogue published during the author's lifetime; and which is our text. See our Preface and Memorial-Introduction for account of other editions, original, early, and modern. G.

THE

SYNAGOGUE,

OR,

THE SHADOW

OF THE

TEMPLE.

Sacred Poems, and
Private Ejaculations.

In imitation of

Mr. George Herbert.

PLIN. SEC. lib. i. Ep. 5.
Stultissimum credo ad imitandum non optima
quæque proponere.

I do esteem't a folly not the least
To imitate examples not the best.

The fourth Edition, corrected
and enlarged.

.

LONDON,
Printed for *Philemon Stephens*, at the guilded
Lyon in St. *Pauls* Church-yard. 1661.

[12mo.]

To the Author.

He that doth imitate must comprehend
Verse, matter, order, titles, spirit, wit ;
For these our Church-Poet doth intend,
And he who hath this Imitation writ.
    O glory of the time ! best English singer !
    Happy both he the hand, and thou the Finger !

R. L[angford of Gray's Inn, Counsellor of Law].

THE SYNAGOGUE.

1. SUBTERLIMINARE.[1]

Dio, cujus Templum? Christi. Quis condidit? Ede.
  Condidit Herbertus. Dic, quibus auxiliis?
Auxiliis multis : quibus haud mihi dicere fas est.
  Tanta est ex dictis lis oriunda meis.
Gratia, si dicam, dedit omnia ; protinus obstat   5
  Ingenium, dicens cuncta fuisse sua.
Ars negat, et nihil est non nostrum dicit in illo ;
  Nec facile est litem composuisse mihi.
Divide : materiam det gratia, materiaeque
  Ingenium cultus induat arsque modos.   10
Non : ne displiceat pariter res omnibus ista,
  Nec sortita velint jura vocare sua.
Nempe pari sibi jure petunt cultusque modosque
  Materiamque ars et gratia et ingenium.
Ergo, velit si quis dubitantem tollere elenchum,   15
  De Templo Herberti talia dicta dabit.
In Templo Herbertus condendo est gratia totus,
  Ars pariter totus, totus et ingenium.
Cedite Romanae, Graiiae quoque cedite Musae ;
  Unum par cunctis Anglia jactat opus.   20

[1] The figures [1], [2], &c., refer to Notes and Illustrations at
p. 90 et seq.   G.

2. A STEPPING-STONE

TO THE THRESHOLD OF MR. HERBERT'S CHURCH-PORCH.

What church is this? Christ's church. Who builded it?
Master George Herbert.   Who assisted it?
Many assisted; who I may not say,
So much contention might arise that way.
If I say Grace gave all, Wit straight doth thwart,[2]   5
And says, 'All that is there is mine;' but Art
Denies, and saies, 'There's nothing there but's mine.'
Nor can I easily the right define.
Divide; say, Grace the matter gave, and Wit
Did polish it: Art measur'd and made fit   10
Each sev'ral piece, and fram'd it altogether.
No, by no means; this may not please them neither:
None's well contented with a part alone,
When each doth challenge all to be his own.
The matter, the expressions, and the measures,   15
Are equally Art's, Wit's, and Grace's treasures.
Then he that would impartially discuss
This doubtful question must answer thus:
In building of his Temple Master Herbert
Is equally all grace, all wit, all art.   20
　　Roman and Grecian Muses, all give way;
　　One English poem darkens all your day.

3. THE DEDICATION.

Lord, my first-fruits should have been sent to Thee ;
    For Thou, the tree
That bare them, only lentest unto me.

But while I had the use, the fruit was mine ;
    Not so divine,   5
As that I dare presume to call it Thine.

Before 'twas ripe it fell unto the ground ;
    And since, I found
It bruisèd in the dirt ; nor clean nor sound.

Some I have pick'd and wip'd, and bring Thee now : 10
    Lord, Thou know'st how
Gladly I would, but dare not it avow.

Such as it is, 'tis here.   Pardon the best ;
    Accept the rest :
Thy pardon and acceptance maketh blest.   15

4. THE CHURCHYARD.

Thou that intendest to the church to-day,
Come, take a turn or two, before thou go'st,
In the Churchyard ; the walk is in thy way.
Who takes best heed in going, hasteth most ;
    But he that unpreparèd rashly ventures   5
    Hastens perhaps to seal his death's indentures.

5. THE CHURCH-STILE.

Seest thou that Stile? Observe, then, how it rises,
Step after step, and equally descends :
Such is the way to win celestial prizes ;
Humility the course begins and ends.
 Wouldst thou in grace to high perfections grow? 5
 Shoot thy roots deep, ground thy foundations low.

Humble thyself, and God will lift thee up ;
Those that exalt themselves He casteth down ;
The hungry He invites with Him to sup,
And cloaths the naked with His robe and crown.   10
 Think not thou hast what thou from Him wouldst
 His labour's lost, if thou thyself canst save. [have;

Pride is the prodigality of grace,
Which casteth all away by griping all ;
Humility is thrift, both keeps its place,   15
And gains by giving ; riseth by its fall :
 To get by giving, and to lose by keeping,
 Is to be sad in mirth, and glad in weeping.

6. THE CHURCH-GATE.

Next to the Stile, see where the Gate doth stand ;
Which, turning upon hooks and hinges, may
Eas'ly be shut or open'd with an hand,
Yet constant to its center still doth stay ;

And fetching a wide compass round about,   5
Keeps the same course and distance, never out.

Such must the course be that to heaven tends;
He that the gates of righteousness would enter
Must still continue constant to his ends,
And fix himself in God, as in his center;   ·   10
    Cleave close to Him by faith; then move which way
    Discretion leads thee, and thou shalt not stray.

We never wander till we loose our hold   = let go
Of Him that is our Way, our Light, our Guide;
But when we grow of our own strength too bold,   15
Unhook'd from Him, we quickly turn aside.
    He holds us up whilst in Him we are found;
    If once we fall from Him, we go to ground.

⁊ 7. THE CHURCH-WALLS.

Now view the Walls; the church is compass'd round
As much for safety as for ornament;
'Tis an inclosure, and no common ground;
'Tis God's free-hold, and but our tenement.
    Tenants at will, and yet in tail,[3] we be;   5
    Our children have the same right to't as we.

Remember there must be no gaps left ope
Where God hath fenc'd, for fear of false illusions.
God will have all, or none; allows no scope
For sin's incroachments or men's own intrusions.   10

Close binding locks His laws together fast ;[4]
He that plucks out the first pulls down the last.

Either resolve for all, or else for none ;
Obedience universal He doth claim.
Either be wholly His, or all thine own ;   15
At what thou canst not reach, at least take aym :
    He that of purpose looks beside the mark
    Might as well hood-winckt[5] shoot, or in the dark.

8. THE CHURCH.

Lastly, consider where the Church doth stand ;
As near unto the middle as may be :
God in His service chiefly doth command
Above all other things sincerity :
    Lines drawn from side to side within a round,   5
    Not meeting in the center, short are found.

Religion must not side with anything
That swerves from God, or else withdraws from Him ;
He that a welcome sacrifice would bring
Must fetch it from the bottom, not the brim :   10
    A sacred temple of the Holy Ghost
    Each part of man must be, but his heart most.

Hypocrisie in church is alchimy,[6]
That casts a golden tincture[7] upon brass ;
There is no essence in it ; 'tis a lye,   15
    Though, fairly stampt, for truth it often pass ;

Only the Spirit's[8] *aqua regia* doth
Discover it to be but painted froth.

9. THE CHURCH-PORCH.

Now, ere thou passest further, sit thee down
In the Church-Porch, and think what thou hast seen;
Let due consideration either crown
Or crush thy former purposes : between
    Rash undertakings and firm resolutions   5
    Depends the strength or weakness of conclusions.

Trace thy steps backward in thy memory;
And first resolve of what thou heardest last,[9]
Sincerity : it blots the history
Of all religious actions, and doth blast   10
    The comfort of them, when in them God sees
    Nothing but outsides of formalities.

In earnest be religious, trifle not,
And rather for God's sake than for thine own;
Thou hast robb'd Him, unless that He have got   15
By giving, if His glory be not grown
    Together with thy good : who seeketh more
    Himself than God would make His roof his floor.

Next to sincerity, remember still
Thou must resolve upon integrity :   20
God will have all thou hast—thy mind, thy will,
Thy thoughts, thy words, thy works. A nullity

It proves, when God, that should have all, doth find
That there is any one thing left behind.

And having giv'n Him all, thou must receive　　25
All that He gives; mete His commandment;
Resolve that thine obedience must not leave
Until it reach unto the same extent:
　　For all His precepts are of equal strength,
　　And measure thy performance to the length.　　30

Then call to mind that constancy must knit
Thine undertakings and thine actions fast:
He that sets forth tow'rds heaven, and doth sit
Down by the way, will be found short at last.
　　Be constant to the end, and thou shalt have　　35
　　An heavenly garland, though an earthly grave.

But he that would be constant must not take
Religion up by fits and starts alone,　　　　=only, merely
But his continual practice must it make;
His course must be from end to end but one:　　40
　　Bones often broken and knit up again　　　　[gain.
　　Lose of their length, though in their strength they

Lastly, remember that humility
Must solidate[10] and keep all close together.
What pride puffs up with vain futility　　45
Lyes open and expos'd to all ill weather;
　　An empty bubble may fair colours carry,
　　But blow upon it, and it will not tarry.

Prize not thine own too high, nor under-rate
Another's worth, but deal indifferently;   50
View the defects of thy spiritual state,
And others' graces, with impartial eye :
    The more thou deemest of thyself, the less
    Esteem of thee will all men else express.

Contract thy lesson now, and this is just   55
The sum of all ;—he that desires to see
The Face of God, in his religion must
Sincere, entire, constant, and humble be.
    If thus resolvèd, fear not to proceed;
    Else the more haste thou mak'st, the worse thou'lt
      speed.   60

10. CHURCH-UTENSILS.

Betwixt two dang'rous rocks, Prophaneness on
Th' one side, on th' other Superstition,
       How shall I sail secure ?
    Lord, be my steersman, hold my helm,
    And then, though winds with waves orewhelm   5
       My sails, I will endure
It patiently.   The bottom of the sea
Is safe enough, if Thou direct the way.

I'll tug my tacklings then, I'll ply mine oars,
And cry, ' A fig for fear !' He that adores   10
       The giddy multitude

So much as to despise my rhymes
Because they tune not to the times,
I wish may not intrude
His presence here.   But they (and that's enough)   15
Who love God's House will like His houshold stuff.

11. THE FONT.

'The Font,' I say.   'Why not?   And why not near
To the church-door?'   'Why not of stone?'
'Is not that blessèd fountain open'd here,
From whence that water flows alone   [Zech. xiii. 1
Which from sin and uncleanness washeth clear?'   5

'And may not beggers well contented be
Their first alms at the door to take?
Though, when acquainted better, they may see
Others within that bolder make :
Low places will serve guests of low degree.'   10

'What!   Is He not the rock, out of whose side
Those streams of water-bloud run forth?   1 Cor. x. 4
Th' elect and precious corner-stone well try'd?
Though th' odds be great between their worth,
Rock-water and stone-vessels are ally'd.'   15

But call it what, and place it where you will,
Let it be made indifferently
Of any form or matter ; yet, untill
The blessèd Sacrament thereby
Impairèd be, my hopes you shall not kill.   20

To want a complement[11] of comliness
    Some of my comfort may abate,
And for the present make my joy go less ;
    Yet I will hug mine homely state,
And poverty with patience richly dress.   25

Regeneration is all in all ;
    Washing or sprinkling but the sign
The seal, and instrument thereof; I call
    The one as well as the other mine,
And my posterity's, as foederal.[12]   30

If temporal estates may be convey'd
    By cov'nants on condition
To men and to their heirs ; be not affraid,
    My soul, to rest upon
The covenant of grace, by Mercy made.   35

Do but thy duty, and rely upon't,
    Repentance, faith, obedience,
Whenever practis'd truly, will amount
    To an authentick evidence,
Though th' deed were antidated at the Font.   40

12. THE READING-PUE.[13]

Here my new-enter'd soul doth first break fast,
    Here seasoneth her infant tast,
And at her mother-nurse the Churche's dugs
    With lab'ring lips and tongue she tugs,

For that sincere milk, which alone doth feed   5
    Babes new-born of immortal seed ;
Who, that they may unto perfection grow,
Must be content to creep before they go.

They that would reading out of church exclude
    Sure have a purpose to obtrude   10
Some dictates of their own, instead of God's
    Revealèd will, His Word.   'Tis odds,
They do not mean to pay men currant coyn,
    Who seek the standard to purloyn,
And would reduce all tryals to their own,   15
But touch-stones, ballances, and weights alone.[14]

What reasonable man would not misdoubt
    Those comments that the text leave out ?
And that their main intent is alteration,
    Who doat so much on variation,   20
That no Set Forms at all they can endure
    To be prescrib'd, or put in ure ?   =use
Rejecting bounds and limits is the way,
If not all waste, yet common all to lay.

But why should he that thinks himself well grown   20
    Be discontent that such a one
As knows himself an infant yet, should be
    Dandled upon his mother's knee,
And babe-like fed with milk, till he have got
    More strength and stomach ?   Why should not   30

Nurslings in church, as well as weanlings, find
Their food fit for them in their proper kind?

Let them that would build castles in the air
    Vault thither without step or stair;
Instead of feet to climbe, take wings to flie,   35
    And think their turrets top[15] the skie.
But let me lay all my foundations deep,
    And learn, before I run, to creep.
Who digs through rocks to lay his ground-works low
May in good time build high and sure, though slow.

To take degrees *per saltum*, though of quick   41
    Dispatch, is but a truant's trick.
Let us learn first to know our letters well,
    Then syllables, then words to spell,
Then to read plainly, e're we take the pen   45
    In hand to write to other men.
I doubt their preaching is not always true
Whose way to th' pulpit's not the Reading-pue.

13. THE BOOK OF COMMON PRAYER.

'What! Pray'r by th' book? and Common?'
                'Yes. Why not?'
      'The Spirit of grace
    And supplication
    Is not left free alone   5
      For time and place;

C

But manner too.' ' To read or speak by rote
    Is all alike to him that praies
    With's heart what with his mouth he saies.'

' They that in private by themselves alone   10
        Do pray, may take
      What liberty they please
      In choosing of the waies
        Wherein to make
Their souls' most intimate affections known   15
    To Him that sees in secret, when
    Th' are most conceal'd from other men.

But he that unto others leads the way
      In publick pray'r
      Should choose to do it so   20
      As all that hear, may know
        They need not fear
To tune their hearts unto his tongue, and say
    Amen ; nor doubt they were betray'd
    To blaspheme, when they should have pray'd. 25

Devotion will adde life unto the letter;
      And why should not
      That which authority
      Prescribes esteemèd be
        Advantage got?   30
If the pray'r be good, the commoner the better ;
    Pray'r in the Churche's words, as well
    As sense, of all pray'rs bears the bell.'[16]

14. THE BIBLE.

The Bible; that's the Book.   The Book indeed,
         The Book of Books ;
         On which who looks,
As he should do, aright, shall never need
         Wish for a better light   5
         To guide him in the night ;

Or, when he hungry is, for better food
         To feed upon
         Than this alone,
If he bring stomach and digestion good ;   10
         And if he be amiss,
         This the best physick is.

The true panchreston[17] 'tis for ev'ry sore
         And sickness, which
         The poor and rich   15
With equal ease may come by : yea, 'tis more ;
         An antidote as well
         As remedy 'gainst hell.

'Tis heaven in perspective ;[18] and the bliss
         Of glory here,   20
         If anywhere,
By saints on earth anticipated is ;
         Whilst faith to ev'ry word
         A being doth afford.

It is the looking-glass of souls, wherein   25
      All men may see
      Whether they be
Still, as by nature th' are, deform'd with sin ;
      Or in a better case,
      As new-adorn'd with grace.   30

'Tis the great magazine of spir'tual arms,
      Wherein doth lye
      Th' artillerie
Of heaven, ready-charg'd against all harms
      That might come by the blowes   35
      Of our infernal foes.

God's cabinet of reveal'd counsel 'tis ;
      Where weal and woe
      Are order'd so,
That every man may know which shall be his ;   40
      Unless his own mistake
      False application make.

It is the index to eternity;   =pointer
      He cannot miss
      Of endless bliss   45
That takes this chart to steer his voyage by;
      Nor can he be mistook
      That speaketh by this book.[19]

A book to which no book may be compar'd
      For excellence ;
      Pre-eminence   50

Is proper to it, and cannot be shar'd;
    Divinity alone
    Belongs to it or none.

It is the Book of God. What if I should   55
    Say, god of books?
    Let him that looks
Angry at that expression, as too bold,
    His thoughts in silence smother
    Till he finds such another.   60

15. THE PULPIT.

    'Tis dinner-time; and now I look
For a full meal. God send me a good cook :[20]
    This is the dresser-bord; and here
I wait in expectation of good chear.
    I'm sure the Master of the house   5
Enough to entertain His guests allows;
And not enough of some one sort alone,
But choyce of what best fitteth every one.

    God grant me taste and stomach good;
My feeding will diversifie my food;   10
    'Tis a good appetite to eat,
And good digestion that makes good meat :
    The best food in itself will be,
Not fed on well, poyson, not food, to me;
Let him that speaks look to his words; my ear   15
Must careful be both what and how I hear.

'Tis manna that I look for here,
The bread of Heaven, Angels' food.   I fear
   No want of plenty, where I know
The loaves by eating more and greater grow;   20
   Where nothing but forbearance makes
A famine; where he only wants that takes
Not what he will; provided that he would
Take nothing to himself but what he should.

   Here the same fountain poureth forth   25
Water, wine, milk, oyl, honey; and the worth
   Of all transcendent, infinite
In excellence, and to each appetite
   In fitness answerable; so
That none needs hence unsatisfièd go,   30
Whose stomach serves him unto any thing
That health, strength, comfort, or content can bring.

   Yea, dead men here invited are
Unto the Bread of life, and whilst they spare
   To come and take it, they must blame   35
Themselves, if they continue still the same.
   The body's fed by food, which it
Assimilates and to itself doth fit;
But that the soul may feed, itself must be
Transformèd to the Word, with it agree.   40

   To milk the strongest men must be
As new-born babes, whenever they it see,

Desiring, not despising it.
For strong meat babes must stay, and strive to fit
    Themselves in time, until they can   45
Get by degrees (which best beseem a man)
Experience-exercisèd senses, able
Good to discern from evill, truth from fable.

    Here I will wait, then, till I see
The steward reaching out a mess for me ;   50
    Resolve I'll take it thankfully,   .
Whate'er it be, and feed on't heartily.
    Although no Benjamin's choice mess,
Five times as much as others', but far less;
Yea, if't be but a basket full of crums,   55
I'll bless the hand from which, by which, it comes.

    Like an invited guest, I will
Be bold, but mannerly withal; sit still
    And see what th' Master of the feast
Will carve unto me, and account that best   60
    Which He doth choose for me, not I
Myself desire : yea, though I should espy
Some fault in th' dressing, in the dishing, or
The placing, yet I will not it abhor.

    So that the meat be wholsome, though   65
The sauce shall not be toothsome,[21] I'll not go
    Empty away, and starve my soul,
To feed my foolish fancy; but controul

My appetite to dainty things,
Which oft, instead of strength, diseases brings ;   70
But if my Pulpit-hopes shall all prove vain,
I'll back unto the reading-pue again.

16. THE COMMUNION-TABLE.

Here stands my banquet ready, the last course
        And best provision,[22]
        That I must feed upon
Till death my soul and body shall divorce
        And that I am   5
Call'd to the marriage-supper of the Lamb.

Some call 't the Altar, some the Holy Table :
        The name I stick not at ;
        Whether 't be this or that,
I care not much, so that I may be able   10
        Truly to know
Both why it is and may be callèd so.

And for the matter whereof it is made,
        The matter is not much,
        Although it be of tuch,[23]   15
Or wood, or mettal, what will last or fade,
        So vanity
And superstition avoided be.

Nor would it trouble me to see it found
        Of any fashion   20
        That can be thought upon,—

Square, oval, many-angled, long, or round;
      If close[24] it be,
Fixt, open, moveable, all's one to me.

And yet, methinks, at a Communion   25
      In uniformity
      There's greatest decency,
And that which maketh most for union;
      But needlessly
To vary tends to th' breach of charity.   30

Yet, rather than I'll give, I will not take
      Offence, if it be given;
      So that[25] I be not driven
To thwart authority, a party make
      For faction,   35
Or side but seemingly in th' action.

At a Communion I wish I might
      Have no cause to suspect
      Any, the least, defect
Of unity and peace, either in sight   40
      Apparently,   = visibly
Or in men's hearts concealèd secretly.

That which ordainèd is to make men one
      More than before they were
      Should not itself appear,   45
Though but appear, distinctly divers.   None
      Too much can see
Of what when most, yet but enough can be.

If others will dissent and vary, who
    Can help it?　If I may,　　　　　50
    As hath been done alway
By th' best and most, I will myself do so:
      Of one accord
The servants should be of one God, one Lord.

17. COMMUNION-PLATE.

Never was gold or silver gracèd thus
    Before:
To bring this Body and this Blood to us
    Is more
      Then to crown kings,　　　　　5
      Or be made rings
For star-like diamonds to glitter in.

No precious stones are meet to match this bread
    Divine;
Spirits of pearls dissolvèd would but dead[26]　　10
    This wine:
    This heav'nly food
    Is too-too good
To be compar'd to any earthly thing.

For such inestimable treasure can　　　　　15
    There be
Vessels too costly made by any man?
    Sure he

That knows the meat
So good to eat   20
Would wish to see it richly servèd in.

Although 'tis true that sanctitie's not ty'd
To state,
Yet sure Religion should not be envy'd
The fate   25
Of meaner worth,
To be set forth
As best becomes the service of a King.

A King unto Whose Cross all kings must vail[27]
Their crowns,   30
And at His beck in their full course strike sail;
Whose frowns
And smiles give date
Unto their fate,
And doom them either unto weal or woe.   35

A King Whose will is justice, and Whose word
Is pow'r
And wisdom both ; a King, Whom to afford
An hour
Of service truly   40
Perform'd and duly,
Is to bespeak eternity of bliss.

When such a King offers to come to me
As food,
Shall I suppose His carriages can be   45

Too good ?
No ; stars to gold
Turn'd, never could
Be rich enough to be employèd so.

If I might wish, then, I would have this bread,   50
This wine,
Vessel'd[28] in what the sun might blush to shed
His shine
When he should see ;
But till that be,   55
I'll rest contented with it as it is.

18. CHURCH-OFFICERS.

Stay—' Officers in church ?'   Take heed : it is
A tender matter to be toucht.
If I chance to say any thing amiss,
Which is not fit to be avoucht,
I must expect whole swarms of waspes to sting me ; 5
Few or no bees, honey or wax to bring me.

Some would have none in church do anything
As Officers but gifted men ;
Others into the number more would bring
Then I see warrant for : so then,   10
All that I say, 'tis like will censur'd be,
Through prejudice or partiality.

But 'tis no matter; if men censure me,
    They but my fellow-servants are :
Our Lord allows us all like liberty.   15
    I write, mine own thoughts to declare,
Not to please men; and if I displease any,
I will not care, so they be of the many.[29]

19. THE SEXTON.

The churche's key-keeper opens the door
        And shuts it, sweeps the floor,
Rings bells, digs graves and fills them up again ;
        All emblems unto men
Openly owning Christianity,   5
To mark, and learn many good lessons by.

O Thou that hast the Key of David, Who
        Open'st and shuttest so
That none can shut or open after Thee,
        Vouchsafe Thyself to be   10
Our souls' doorkeeper by Thy blessèd Spirit ;
The lock and key's Thy mercy, not our merit.

Cleanse Thou our sin-soyl'd souls from th' dirt and dust
        Of every noysome lust
Brought in by the foul feet of our affections;   15
        The beesome[30] of afflictions,
With th' blessing of Thy Spirit added to it,
If Thou be pleas'd to say it shall, will do it.

Lord, ringing changes all our bells hath marr'd,
　　　　Jangled they have and jarr'd　　　　　20
So long, they're out of tune and out of frame;
　　　　They seem not now the same.
Put them in frame anew, and once begin
To tune[31] them so, that they may chime all in.

Let all our sins be buri'd in Thy grave,　　　　25
　　　　No longer rant and rave,
As they have done, to our eternal shame,
　　　　And th' scandal of Thy name.
Let's as door-keepers in Thine house attend,　Ps. lxxxiv. 10
Rather than th' throne of wickedness ascend.　　30

20. THE CLERK.

The churche's Bible-Cleark attends
　　　　Her utensils, and ends
　　　　Her prayers with Amen;
Tunes Psalms, and to the Sacraments
　　　　Brings in the elements,　　　　5
　　　　And takes them out again;
Is humble-minded and industrious-handed;
Doth nothing of himself, but as commanded.

All that the vessels of the Lord
　　　　Do bear, with one accord　　　　10
　　　　Must study to be pure

As they are : if His holy eye
    Do any spot espy,
    He cannot it endure,
But most expecteth to be sanctifi'd[32]   15
In those come nearest Him, and glorifi'd.

    Psalms then are alwaies tunèd best
        When there is most exprest
        The holy penman's heart ;
    All musick is but discord where   20
        That wants, or doth not bear
        The first and chiefest part :
Voices without affections answerable,
When best, to God are most abominable.

    Though in the blessèd Sacraments   25
        The outward elements
        Are but as husks and shells,
    Yet he that knows the kernel's worth,
        If even those send forth
        Some aromatick smels,[33]   30
Will not esteem it waste, lest, Judas-like,
Through Marie's side he Christ Himself should strike.

    Lord, without Whom we cannot tell
        How to speak or think well,
        Lend us Thy helping hand,   35
    That what we do may pleasing be,
        Not to ourselves, but Thee,
        And answer Thy command :   =agree with

So that, not we alone, but Thou mayst say
Amen to all our pray'rs, pray'd the right way.   40

21. THE OVERSEER OF THE POOR.

The Churche's Almoner takes care that none
       In their necessity
       Shall unprovided be
Of maint'nance or imployment; those alone
       Whom careless idleness   5
       Or riotous excess
Condemns to needless want, he leaves to be
Chasten'd a while by their own povertie.

Thou, gracious Lord, rich in Thyself, dost give
       To all men lib'rally,   10
       Upbraiding none; Thine eye
Is open upon all; in Thee we live,
       We move, and have our being :
       But there is more than seeing
For th' poor with Thee; they are Thy special charge; 15
To them Thou dost Thine heart and hand enlarge.[34]

Four sorts of poor there are, with whom Thou deal'st—
       Though alwaies diff'rently—
       With such indiff'rency,   =impartiality
That none hath reason to complain; Thou heal'st   20
       All those whom Thou dost wound ;
       If there be any found

Hurt by themselves, Thou leav'st them to endure
The pain, till th' pain render them fit for cure.

Some in the world are poor, but rich in faith; 25
        Their outward poverty   St. James ii. 5
        A plentiful supply
Of inward comforts and contentments hath ;
        And their estate is blest
        In this above the rest,— 30
It was Thy choice whilst Thou on earth didst stay,
And hadst not whereupon Thy head to lay.

Some 'poor in spirit' in the world are rich,
        Although not many such ;
        And no man needs to grutch 35
Their happiness, who to maintain that pitch
        Have an hard task in hand,
        Nor eas'ly can withstand
The strong temptations that attend on riches :
Mountains are more expos'd to storms than ditches. 40

Some rich in th' world are spiritually poor,
        And destitute of grace ;
        Who may perchance have place
In the church upon earth ; but Heaven's door
        Too narrow is t' admit 45
        Such camels in at it,
Till they sell all they have, that field to buy
Wherein the true treasure doth hidden lye.   Matt. xiii. 44

D

Some sp'ritually poor and destitute
     Of grace in th' world are poor,   50
     Begging from door to door,
Accursèd both in God's and man's repute;
     Till, by their miseries
     Tutor'd, they learn to prize
Hungring and thirsting after righteousness,   55
Whilst they're on earth, their greatest happiness.

Lord, make me ' poor in spirit,' and relieve
     Me how Thou wilt Thyself;
     No want of worldly pelf
Shall make me discontented, fret, and grieve.   60
     I know Thine alms are best;
     But, above all the rest,
Condemn me not unto the hell of riches,
Without Thy grace to countercharme[35] the witches.

22. THE CHURCHWARDEN.

The Churche's Guardian takes care to keep
     Her buildings alwaies in repaire;
Unwilling that any decay should creep
     On them before he is aware :
     Nothing defac'd,   5
     Nothing displac'd
He likes; but most doth long and love to see
The living stones order'd as they should be.

Lord, Thou not only Supervisor art
    Of all our works, but in all those   10
Which we dare own, Thine is the chiefest part;
    For there is none of us that knows
        How to do well;
        Nor can we tell
What we should do, unless by Thee directed :   15
It prospers not that's by ourselves projected.

That which we think ourselves to mend, we mar,
    And often make it ten times worse;
Reforming of religïon by war
    Is th' chymick blessing[36] of a curse.   20
        Great odds it is
        That we shall miss
Of what we lookèd for; Thine ends cannot
By any but by Thine own means be got.

'Tis strange we so much dote upon our own   25
    Deformity, and others scorn,
As if ourselves were beautiful alone;
    When that which did us most adorn
        We purposely
        Choose to lay by,   30
Such decency and order as did place us
In high'st esteem, and guard as well as grace us.

Is not Thy daughter glorious within,   Ps. xlv. 13, 14
    When cloath'd in needle-work without?
Or is't not rather both their shame and sin   35

That change her robe into a clout
     Too narrow and
     Too thin to stand
Her need in any stead, much less to be
An ornament fit for her high degree?   40

Take pity on her, Lord, and heal her breaches;
     Clothe all her enemies with shame;
All the despight that's done unto her reaches
     To the dishonour of Thy name.
         Make all her sons   45
         Rich precious stones,
To shine each of them in his proper place,
Receiving of Thy fulness grace for grace.

23. THE DEACON.

'The Deacon!   That's the minister.'
     'True, taken gen'rally,[37]
     And without any sinister
         Intent, us'd specially;
He's purposly ordain'd to minister   5
In sacred things t' another officer.

At whose appointment, in whose stead,
     He doth what he should do
In some things, not in all; is led
     By law and custom too;   10
Where that doth neither bid nor forbid, he
Thinks this sufficient authority.

Loves not to vary, when he sees
    No great necessitie ;
To what's commanded he agrees   15
    With all humility ;
Knowing how highly God submission prizes,
Pleas'd with obedience more than sacrifices.'   1 Sam. xv. 22

Lord, Thou didst of Thyself profess
    Thou wast as one that serv'd,   20
And freely choosest to go less,   St. Luke xxii. 27
    Though none so much deserv'd.
With what face can we, then, refuse to be
Entred Thy servants in a low degree ?

Thy way to exaltation   25
    Was by humilitie ;
But we, proud generation,
    No diff'rence of degree
In holy orders will allow ; nay more,
All holy orders would turn out of door.   30

But if Thy precept cannot do't,
    To make us humbly serve,
Nor Thy example added to't,
    If still from both we swerve ;
Let none of us proceed,[38] till he can tell   35
How t' use the office of a deacon well.

Which by the blessing of Thy Spirit,
    Whom Thou hast left to be

Thy vicar here, we may inherit,
    And minister to Thee,   40
Though not so well as Thou mayst well expect,
Yet so as Thou wilt pleasèd be t' accept.

24. THE PRIEST.

The Priest I say; the Presbyter I mean,
    As now-a-daies he's call'd
By many men; but I choose to retain
    The name wherewith instal'd
He was at first in our own mother-tongue;   5
And doing so, I hope I do no wrong.

The Priest, I say, 's a middle-officer
    Between the bishop and
The deacon; as a middle-offerer,
    Which in the church doth stand   10
Between God and the people, ready prest,[39]
In the behalf of both to do his best.

From Him to them offers the promises
    Of mercy which He makes;
For them to Him doth all their faults confess;   15
    Their prayers and praises takes,
And offers for them at the throne of grace,
Contentedly attending his own place.   =awaiting

The Word and Sacraments, the means of grace,
    He duly doth dispence,   20

The flourishes of falshood to deface
    With truth's clear evidence,
And sin's usurpèd tyranny suppress
B' advancing righteousness and holiness.

The publick censures [40] of the Church he sees   25
    To execution brought;
But nothing rashly of himself decrees,
    Nor covets to be thought
Wiser than his superiours; whom alwaies
He actively or passively obeys.   30

Lord Jesus, Thou the Mediator art
    Of the New Testament,
And fully didst perform Thy double part
    Of God and man, when sent
To reconcile the world, and to attone[41]   35
'Twixt it and heaven, of two making one.

Yea, after the order of Melchisedeck   Ps. cx. 4
    Thou art a Priest for ever;
With perfect righteousness Thyself dost deck,
    Such as decayeth never.   40
Like to Thyself make all Thy priests on earth,
Bless'd fathers to Thy sons of th' second birth.

Thou cam'st to do the will of Him that sent Thee,
    And didst His honour seek
More than Thine own; well may it, then, repent Thee,
    Being Thyself so meek,   46

To have admitted them into the place
Of sons, that seek their fathers to disgrace.

Lord, grant that the abuse may be reform'd
   Before it ruine bring   50
Upon Thy poor despisèd Church, transform'd
   As if 'twere no such thing ;
Thou that the God of order art, and peace,
Make curs'd confusion and contention cease.

25. THE BISHOP.

' The Bishop ?' ' Yes, why not ? What doth that name
Import that is unlawful or unfit ?
To say the Overseer is the same
In substance, and no hurt, I hope, in it ;
  But sure if men did not despise the thing, 5
  Such scorn upon the name they would not fling.

Some priests—some presbyters I mean—would be
Each overseer of his sev'ral cure ;
But one superiour, to oversee
Them altogether, they will not endure :   10
  This the main diff'rence is that I can see,—
  Bishops they would not have, but they would be.

But who can show of old that ever any
Presbyteries without their bishops were ?
Though bishops without presbyteries many[42] 15
At first must needs be almost every where ;

That presbyters from bishops first arose,
T' assist them, 's probable, not these from those.

However, a true bishop I esteem
The highest officer the Church on earth   20
Can have, as proper to itself, and deem
A Church without one an imperfect birth,
    If constituted so at first ; and maim'd,
    If whom it had, it afterwards disclaim'd.

All order first from unity ariseth,   25
And th' essence of it is subordination ;
Whoever this contemns, and that despiseth,
May talk of, but intends not, reformation :
    'Tis not of God, of nature, or of art,
    T' ascribe to all what's proper to one part.   30

To rule, and to be ruled, are distinct ;
And sev'ral duties sev'rally belong
To sev'ral persons,[43] can no more be linkt
In altogether, than amidst the throng
    Of rude unruly passions in the heart,   35
    Reason can see to act her soveraign part.

But a good bishop, as a tender father,
Doth teach and rule the Church, and is obey'd
And reverenc'd by it ; so much the rather,
By how much he delighteth more to lead   40
    All by his own example in the way,
    Then punish any when they go astray.

Lord, Thou the Bishop and Chief Shepherd art
Of all that flock which Thou hast purchasèd
With Thine own bloud ; to them Thou dost impart 45
The benefits which Thou hast merited,
  Teaching and ruling, by Thy blessèd Spirit,
  Their souls in grace, till glory they inherit.

The stars which Thou dost hold in Thy right hand,
The angels of the churches, Lord, direct   Rev. i. 16 50
Clearly Thy holy will to understand,
And do accordingly : let no defect
  Nor fault, no not in our new politicks,
  Provoke Thee to remove our candlesticks ;

But let Thy Urim and Thy Thummim be   55
Garments of praise t' adorn Thine holy ones ;
Light and perfection let all men see
Brightly shine forth in those rich precious stones,
  Of whom Thou wilt make a foundation,
  To raise Thy new Hierusalem upon.   60

And, at the brightness of its rising, let
All nations with Thy people shout for joy ;
Salvation for walls and bulwarks set
About it, that nothing may it annoy.
  Then the whole world Thy diocess shall be,   65
  And bishops all but suffragans to Thee.'
                    [Ezra iii. 12, 13; Neh. xii. 43; Job xxxviii. 7

26. CHURCH-FESTIVALS.

Marrow of time ; eternity in brief
Compendiums epitomis'd ; the chief
Contents, the indices, the title-pages
Of all past, present, and succeeding ages ;
Sublimate graces, antidated glories ;   5
   The cream of holiness ;
    The inventories
   Of future blessedness ;
The florilegia[44] of celestial stories ;
Spirits of joys ; the relishes and closes   10
Of angels' musick ; pearls dissolvèd ; roses
Perfumèd ; sugar'd honey-combs ; delights
   Never too highly priz'd ;
    The marriage rites,
    Which, duly solemniz'd,   15
Usher espousèd souls to bridal nights ;
Gilded sunbeams ; refinèd elixirs,
And quintessential extracts of stars ;—
Who loves not you, doth but in vain profess
That he loves God, or heaven, or happiness.[45]   20

27. THE SABBATH, OR LORD'S DAY.[46]

Haile,	Vaile
Holy	Wholly
King of daies,	To thy praise,
The emperour,	For evermore

Or universal
Monarch of time, the week's
Perpetual dictatour.
Thy
Beauty
Far exceeds
The reach of art
To blazon⁴⁷ fully;
And I thy light eclipse,
When I most strive to raise
　　　　　[thee.
What
Nothing
Else can be,
Thou only art;
Th' extracted spirit
Of all eternity,
By favour antidated.

Must the rehersal　5
Of all that honour seeks,
Under the world's Crea-
My　　　　　[tour.
Duty
Yet must needs　10
Yield thee mine heart,
And that not dully;
Spirits of souls, not lips
Alone, are fit to praise
　　　　　[thee.
That　15
Slow thing
Time by thee
Hath got the start,
And doth inherit
That immortality　20
Which sin anticipated.

O
That I
Could lay by
This body so,　　　　　25
That my soul might be
Incorporate with thee,
And no more to six daies owe!

28. THE ANNUNCIATION, OR LADY-DAY.

Unto the musick of the sphears
Let men and angels joyn in consort[48] theirs.
    So great a messenger
      From heaven to earth
      Is seldom seen   5
    Attir'd in so much glory;
    A message welcomer,
      Fraught with more mirth,
      Hath never been
    Subject of any story.   10
This by a double right, if any, may
    Be truly stil'd the world's birthday.

The making of the world ne'er cost
So dear, by much as to redeem it lost.
    God said but 'Let it be,'   15
      And ev'ry thing
      Was made straightway
    So as He saw it good;
    But ere that He could see
      A course to bring   20
      Man, gone astray,
    To the place where he stood,
His wisdom with His mercy, for man's sake,
    Against His justice part did take.

And the result was this daie's news,   25
Able the messenger himself t' amuse,[49]

As well as her, to whom
   By him 'twas told   St. Luke,i. 34
   That though she were
A Virgin pure, and knew   30
No man, yet in her womb
A Son she should
Conceive and bear,
As sure as God was true;
Such high place in His favour she possessèd,   35
Being among all women blessèd.

But blest especially in this,
That she believ'd; and for eternal bliss
   Reli'd on Him Whom she
      Herself should bear,   40
   And her own Son
   Took for her Saviour.
   And if there any be, ·
      That when they hear—
      As she had done—   45
   Sute their behaviour,   St. Luke i. 38
They may be blessèd as she was, and say,
'Tis their Annunciation-day.   St. Luke xi. 48

29. THE NATIVITY, OR CHRISTMAS-DAY.[50]

Unfold thy face, unmask thy ray,
Shine forth, bright sun,[51] double the day;
Let no malignant misty fume,
Nor foggy vapour, once presume

To interpose thy perfect sight   5
This day, which makes us love thy light
For ever better, that we could[52]
That blessèd object once behold,
Which is both the circumference
And centre of all excellence ;   10
Or rather neither, but a treasure
Unconfinèd, without measure ;
Whose center and circumference—
Including all preheminence,
Excluding nothing but defect,   15
And infinite in each respect—
Is equally both here and there,
And now, and then, and every where,
And always one, Himself the same,
A Being far above a name.   20
Draw nearer, then, and freely poure
Forth all thy light into that houre
Which was crownèd with His birth,
And made heaven envy earth.

    Let not His birthday clouded be   25
    By Whom thou shinest, and we see.

30. THE CIRCUMCISION, OR NEW YEAR'S-DAY.

Sorrow betide my sins ! Must smart so soon
Scize on my Saviour's tender flesh, scarce grown
    Unto an eighth-daie's age ?
    Can nothing else asswage

The wrath of Heaven but His infant blood ?   5
Innocent Infant, infinitely good !

Is this Thy welcome to the world, great God ?
No sooner born but subject to the rod
      Of sin-incensèd wrath ?
      Alas, what pleasure hath   10
Thy Father's justice to begin Thy passion
Almost together with Thine incarnation ?

Is it to antidate Thy death ? t' indite
Thy condemnation Himself, and write
      The copy[53] with Thy bloud,   15
      Since nothing is so good ?
Or is't by this experiment to try
Whether Thou beest born mortal and canst die ?

If man must needs draw bloud of God, yet why
Stayes he not till Thy time be come to die ?   20
      Didst Thou thus early bleed
      For us to show what need   Rom. ii. 29 ; Phil. iii. 3
We have to hasten unto Thee as fast,
And learn that all the time is lost that's past ?

'Tis true we should do so : yet in this bloud   25
There's something else that must be understood :
      It seals Thy covenant,
      That so we may not want
Witness enough against Thee that Thou art
Made subject to the Law, to act our part.   30

The sacrament of Thy regeneration
It cannot be; it gives no intimation
  Of what Thou wert, but we :[54]
  Native impurity,
Original corruption, was not Thine,   35
But only as Thy righteousness is mine.

In holy Baptism this is brought to me,
As that in Circumcision was to Thee;
  So that Thy loss and pain
  Do prove my joy and gain.   40
Thy circumcision writ Thy death in bloud;
Baptism in water seals my livelihood.[55]

O blessèd change ! Yet, rightly understood,
That bloud was water, and this water's bloud.[56]
  What shall I give again   45
  To recompence Thy pain ?
Lord, take revenge upon me for this smart;
To quit[57] Thy foreskin, circumcise my heart.[58] Rom. ii. 29

31. THE EPIPHANY, OR TWELFTH-DAY.

Great, without controversie great,
  They that do know it will confess
  The ' mystery of godliness,'   1 Tim. iii. 16
Whereof the Gospel doth intreat.

God in the flesh is manifest,   5
  And that which hath for ever been

E

Invisible may now be seen—
  Th' eternal Deity new drest.

Angels to shepherds brought the news ;
  And wise men, guided by a star   10
  To seek the sun, are come from far:
Gentiles have got the start of Jews.   Ma.. iv. 2

The stable and the manger hide
  His glory from His own ; but these,
  Though strangers, His resplendent rayes   15
Of majesty divine have spy'd.

Gold, frankincense, and myrrhe they give;
  And worshipping Him plainly show
  That unto Him they all things owe,
By Whose free gift it is they live.   20

Though clouded in a vail of flesh,
  The Sun of Righteousness appears,
  Melting cold cares and frosty fears,
And making joyes spring up afresh.

O that His light and influence   25
  Would work effectually in me
  Another new Epiphany,
Exhale and elevate me hence !   = draw out

That, as my calling doth require,
  Star-like I may to others shine,   30
  And guide them to that Sun divine
Whose daylight never shall expire.

32. THE PASSION, OR GOOD FRYDAY.

This day my Saviour dy'd : and do I live?
    What, hath not sorrow slain me yet?
Did the immortal God vouchsafe to give
    His life for mine, and do I set
More by my wretched life than He by His,   5
So full of glory and of bliss?

Did His free mercy and meer love to me
    Make Him forsake His glorious throne
And mount a cross, the stage of infamy,
    That so He might not die alone,   Mark xv. 27 10
But dying suffer more through grief and shame
Than mortal men have pow'r to name?

And can ingratitude so far prevail
    To keep me living still? Alas,
Methinks some thorn out of His crown, some nail, 15
    At least His spear, might pierce and pass
Thorow and thorow till it riev'd mine heart,
As the right death-deserving part.

And doth He not expect it should be so?
    Would He lay down a price so great,   20
And not look that His purchases should grow
    Accordingly? Shall I defeat
His just desire? O no, it cannot be;
His death must needs be death to me.

My life's not mine, but His; for He did die   25
    That I might live; yet dièd so,
That being dead He was alive; and I
    Thorow the gates of death must go
To live with Him; yea, to live by Him here
Is a part in His death to bear.   Rom. vi. 3-6   30

Die then, dull soul; and if thou canst not die,
    Dissolve thyself into a sea
Of living tears; whose streams may ne'r go dry,
    Nor turnèd be another way,
Till they have drown'd all joyes but those alone   35
Which Sorrow claimeth for its own.

For sorrow hath its joyes; and I am glad
    That I would grieve if I do not;[59]
But if I neither could nor would be sad
    And sorrowful this day, my lot   40
Would be to grieve for ever with a grief
Uncapable of all relief.

No grief was like that which He griev'd for me,
    A greater grief than can be told;
And like my grief for Him no grief should be,   45
    If I could grieve so as I would;
But what I would, and cannot, He doth see,
And will accept, that dy'd for me.

Lord, as Thy grief and death for me are mine—
    For Thou hast given them unto me—   50

So my desires to grieve and die are Thine,
  For they are wrought only by Thee.
Not for my sake, then, but Thine own, be pleas'd
With that which Thou Thyself hast rais'd.

33. THE RESURRECTION, OR EASTER-DAY.

Up, and away ;
      Thy Saviour's gone before :
Why dost thou stay,
      Dull soul? Behold, the door
Is open, and His precept bids thee rise,   5
Whose pow'r hath vanquisht all thine enemies.

Say not, I live,
      Whilst in the grave thou ly'st :   Col. ii. 13
He that doth give
      Thee life would have thee prize 't   10
More highly than to keep it buri'd where
Thou canst not make the fruits of it appear.

Is rottenness
      And dust so pleasant to thee,
That happiness   15
      And heaven cannot wooe thee
To shake thy shackles off, and leave behind thee
Those fetters which to death and hell do bind thee?

In vain thou say'st
      Thou'rt bury'd with thy Saviour,   20
If thou delay'st

To show by thy behaviour
That thou art risen with Him : till thou shine
Like Him, how canst thou say His light is thine?

[Col. ii. 12

Early He rose,   25
   And with Him brought the day,
Which all thy foes
   Frighted out of the way;
And wilt thou sluggard-like turn in thy bed,
Till noon-sun beams draw up thy drowsie head?   30

[Proverbs vi. 9

Open thine eyes,
   Sin-seisèd[60] soul, and see
What cobweb-tyes
   They are that trammel thee;
Not profits, pleasures, honours, as thou thinkest,   35
But loss, pain, shame, at which thou vainly winkest.

All that is good
   Thy Saviour dearly bought
With His heart's bloud;
   And it must there be sought,   40
Where He keeps residence Who rose this day :
Linger no longer, then; up, and away.

34. THE ASCENTION, OR HOLY THURSDAY.

Mount, mount, my soul, and climbe, or rather flye,
   With all thy force on high :

Thy Saviour rose not only, but ascended;
  And He must be attended
Both in His conquest and His triumph too.   5
  His glories strongly wooe
His graces to them, and will not appear
In their full lustre untill both be there

Where He now sits, not for Himself alone,
  But that upon His throne   10
All His redeemèd may attendants be,
  Robèd and crown'd as He.
Kings without courtiers are 'lone men, they say;
  And do'st thou think to stay
Behind on earth, whilst thy King reigns in heaven, 15
Yet not be of thy happiness bereaven?

Nothing that thou canst think worth having's here;
  Nothing is wanting there
That thou canst wish to make thee truly blest;
  And, above all the rest,   20
Thy life is hid with God in Jesus Christ,   Col. iii. 3
  Higher than what is high'st.
O grovel, then, no longer here on earth,   Heb. i. 4, &c.
Where mis'ry every moment drowns thy mirth.

But tour,[61] my soul, and soar above the skyes,   25
  Where thy true treasure lies:
Though with corruption and mortality
  Thou clogg'd and pinion'd be,

Yet thy fleet thoughts and sprightly wishes may
   Speedily glide away.   30
To what thou canst not reach, at least aspire ;
Ascend, if not in deed, yet in desire.

35. WHIT-SUNDAY.

Nay, startle not to hear that rushing wind,
   Wherewith this place is shaken ;[62]
Attend a while, and thou shalt quickly find
   How much thou art mistaken,
     If thou think here   5
    Is any cause of fear.   .

Seest thou not how on those twelve rev'rend heads
   Sit cloven tongues of fire?
And as the rumor of that wonder spreads,
   The multitude admire   =wonder 10
    To see it, and
    Yet more amazèd stand

To hear at once so great variety
   Of language from them come,
Of whom they dare be bold to say they be   15
   Bred nowhere but at home,
    And never were
    In place such words to hear.

Mock not, prophane despisers of the Spirit,
   At what's to you unknown ;   20

This earnest[63] He hath sent, Who must inherit
    All nations as His own;
        That they may know
        How much to Him they owe.

Now that He is ascended up on high   25
    To His celestial throne,
And hath led captive all captivity,
        He'll not receive alone,
        But likewise give
        Gifts unto all that live,—   30

To all that live by Him, that they may be,
    In His due time, each one
Partakers with Him in His victory;
        Nor He triumph alone,
        But take all His   35
        Unto Him where He is.

To fit them for which blessèd state of glory,
    This is His Agent here;
To publish to the world that happy story,
        Alwaies and everywhere,   40
        This resident
        Embassadour is sent,

Heaven's legier[64] upon earth, to counter-work
    The mines that Satan made,
And bring to light those enemies that lurk   45
        Under sin's gloomy shade;

That hell may not
Still boast what it hath got.

Thus Babel's curse, confusion, is retriev'd ;
      Diversity of tongues   50
By this division of the Sp'rit reliev'd ;
      And to prevent all wrongs,
      One faith unites
      People of different rites.

O let His intertainment, then, be such   55
      As doth Him best befit !
Whatever He requireth, think not much
      Freely to yield Him it ;
      For who doth this
      Reaps the first-fruits of bliss.   60

36. TRINITY SUNDAY.

Grace, wit, and art, assist me ; for I see
The subject of this daie's solemnity
      So far excels in worth,
            That sooner may
            I drain the sea,   5
            Or drive the day
            With light away,
      Than fully set it forth ;
Except you joyn all three to take my part,
And chiefly grace fill both my head and heart. 10

Stay, busie soul, presume not to enquire
Too much of what angels can but admire,   wonder at
  And never comprehend ;
   The Trinity
   In Unity,   15
   And Unity
   In Trinity,
  All reason doth transcend.[65]
God Father, Son God, and God Holy Ghost,
Who most admireth magnificth most.   20

And who most magnifies best understands,
And best expresseth what the heads and hands
  And hearts of all men living,
   When most they try
   To glorifie,   25
   And raise on high,
   Fall short, and lie
  Groveling below : man's giving
Is but restoring by retail, with loss,
What from his God he first receiv'd in gross.[66] 30

Faith must perform the office of invention,
And elocution, struck with apprehension
  Of wonder, silence keep ;
   Not tongues, but eyes
   Lift[67] to the skies   35
   In reverend wise
   Best solemnise

This day; whereof the deep
Mysterious subject lies out of the reach
Of wit to learn, much more of art to teach.   40

Then write *non ultra* here; look not for leave
To speak of what thou never canst conceive
      Worthily as thou shouldest;
          And it shall be
          Enough for thee,   45
          If none but He
          Himself doth see,
      Though thou canst not, thou wouldest
Make His praise glorious, Who is alone
Thrice-blessèd One in Three, and Three in One.   50

37. INVITATION.

Turn in, my Lord, turn in to me;
    Mine heart's a homely place,
But Thou canst make corruption flee,
    And fill it with Thy grace:
So furnishèd it will be brave,   5
And a rich dwelling Thou shalt have.

It was Thy lodging once before;
    It buildèd was by Thee;
But I to sin set ope the door,
    It render'd was by me;   *given up* 10
And so Thy building was defac'd,
And in Thy room another plac'd.

But he usurps, the right is Thine :
    O dispossess him, Lord ;
Do Thou but say, 'This heart is Mine,'   15
    He's gone at the first word ;
Thy word's Thy will, Thy will's Thy power ;
Thy time is alwaies, now's mine hour.

    Now say to sin, 'Depart;'
    And, 'Son, give Me thine heart.'   20
Thou, that by saying 'Let it be,' didst make it,
Canst, if Thou wilt, by saying 'Give't Me,' take it.

38. COMFORT IN EXTREMITY.

Alas, my Lord is going,
    O my woe !
It will be mine undoing ;
    If He go,
I'll run and overtake Him ;   5
    If He stay,
I'll cry aloud, and make Him
    Look this way.
O stay, my Lord, my Love, 'tis I ;
Comfort me quickly, or I dye.   10

'Cheer up thy drooping spirits,
    I am here ;
Mine all-sufficient merits
    Shall appear

Before the throne of glory   15
    In thy stead :
I'll put into thy story
    What I did.
Lift up thine eyes, sad soul, and see
Thy Saviour here : lo, I am He.'   20

Alas, shall I present
    My sinfulness
To Thee? Thou wilt resent
    The loathsomness.
' Be not afraid, I'll take   25
    Thy sins on Me,
And all My favour make
    To shine on thee.'
Lord, what Thou'lt have me Thou must make me.
' As I have made thee now, I take thee.'   30

39. RESOLUTION AND ASSURANCE.

Lord, Thou wilt love me ; wilt Thou not?
    Beshrew[68] that ' not' !
    It was my sin begot
That question first.   Yes, Lord, Thou wilt :
    Thy bloud was spilt   5
    To wash away my guilt.
Lord, I will love Thee; shall I not?
    Beshrew that ' not' !
    'Twas Death's accursèd plot

To put that question.   Yes, I will,   10
   Lord, love Thee still,
  In spite of all my ill.
Then life and love continue still
   We shall and will,
  My Lord and I, untill   15
  In His celestial hill
   We love our fill,
When He hath purgèd all mine ill.

40. VOWS BROKEN AND RENEWED.

Said I not so, that I would sin no more?
  Witness, my God, I did :
Yet I am run again upon the score ;[69]
  My faults cannot be hid.
What shall I do? Make vows, and break them still? 5
  'Twill be but labour lost :
My good cannot prevail against mine ill ;
  The bus'ness will be crost.

O say not so; thou canst not tell what strength
 Thy God may give thee at the length :   10
Renew thy vows, and if thou keep the last,
 Thy God will pardon all that's past.   [mayst
Vow whilst thou canst, while thou canst vow : thou
Perhaps perform it when thou thinkest least.

  Thy God hath not deny'd thee all,   15
  Whilst He permits thee but to call :

Call to thy God for grace to keep
Thy vows; and if thou break them, weep;
Weep for thy broken vows, and vow again;
Vows made with tears cannot be still in vain.   20
　　　Then once again
　　　I vow to mend my ways;
　　　　Lord, say Amen,
　　　　And Thine be all the praise.

41. CONFUSION.

O how my mind
　　　Is gravell'd ![70]
　　　　Not a thought
That I can find
　　　But's ravel'd   5
　　　　All to nought.
Short ends of threds,
　　　And narrow shreds
　　　　Of lists,
Knot-snarl'd ruffs,[71]   10
　　　Loose broken tufts
　　　　Of twists,
Are my torn meditation's ragged clothing;
Which, wound and woven, shape a sute for nothing;
One while I think, and then I am in pain   15
To think how to unthink that thought again.

How can my soul
　　　But famish

With this food?
Pleasure's full bowl   20
    Tastes rammish,[72]
      Taints the blood;
Profit picks bones,
    And chews on stones
      That choak;   25
Honour climbs hills,
    Fats not, but fills
      With smoak.
And whilst my thoughts are greedy upon these,
They pass by pearls, and stoop to pick up pease.   30
Such wash and draff[73] is fit for none but swine:
And such I am not, Lord, if I am Thine.
    Cloath me anew, and feed me then afresh;
    Else my soul dies famisht and starv'd with flesh.

42. A PARADOX:

THE WORSE THE BETTER.

Welcome, mine health; this sickness makes me well.
    Med'cins, adieu:
When with diseases I have list[74] to dwell,
    I'll wish for you.

Welcome, my strength; this weakness makes me able; 5
    Powers, adieu:
When I am weary grown of standing stable,
    I'll wish for you.

F

Welcome, my wealth; this loss hath gain'd me more.
 Riches, adieu: 10
When I again grow greedy to be poor,
  I'll wish for you.

Welcome, my credit; this disgrace is glory.
  Honours, adieu:
When for renown and fame I shall be sorry,[75]   15
  I'll wish for you.

Welcome, content; this sorrow is my joy.
  Pleasures, adieu:
When I desire such griefs as may annoy,
    I'll wish for you.   20

Health, strength, and riches, credit and content,
Are sparèd best sometimes when they are spent;
Sickness and weakness, loss, disgrace, and sorrow,
Lend most sometimes when they seem most to borrow.
Blest be that hand that helps by hurting, gives   25
By taking, by forsaking me relieves.
If in my fall my rising be Thy will,
Lord, I will say, 'The worse the better still.'
I'll speak the paradox; maintain Thou it,
And let Thy grace supply my want of wit.   30
  Leave me no learning that a man may see,
  So I may be a scholar unto Thee.

43. INMATES.

A house I had (an heart, I mean) so wide
And full of spacious rooms on every side,

That, viewing it, I thought I might do well,
Rather than keep it void, and make no gain
Of what I could not use, to entertain   5
    Such guests as came. I did; but what befel
    Me quickly in that course I sigh to tell.

A guest I had—alas, I have her still—
A great big-belly'd guest; enough to fill
    The vast content of hell,—Corruption.   10
By entertaining her I lost my right
To more than all the world hath now in sight;
    Each day, each hour almost, she brought forth one
    Or other base-begot Transgression.

The charge grew great.   I, that had lost before   15
All that I had, was forcèd now to score[76]
    For all the charges of their maintenance
In Dooms-day book.   Whoever knew't would say,
The least sum there was more than I could pay
    When first 'twas due,—besides continuance,   20
    Which could not chuse but much the debt enhance.

To ease me, first I wisht her to remove;
But she would not.   I su'd her then above,
    And begg'd the Court of Heaven, but in vain,
To cast her out.   No, I could not evade   25
The bargain which she pleaded I had made,
    That whilst both livèd I should entertain
    At mine own charge both her and all her train.

No help then, but or I must dye or she ;
And yet my death of no availe would be,   30
    For one death I had dy'd already, then
When first she liv'd in me ; and now to dye
Another death again were but to tye
      And twist them both into a third,[77] which, when
      It once hath seiz'd on, never looseth men.   35

Her death might be my life ; but her to kill
I of myself had neither power nor will:
    So desp'rate was my case.   Whilst I delay'd,
My guest still teem'd, my debts still greater grew ;
The less I had to pay, the more was due.   [=bore 40
      The more I knew, the more I was afraid ;
      The more I mus'd, the more I was dismai'd.

At last I learn'd there was no way but one :
A friend must do it for me.   He alone,
    That is the Lord of life, by dying can   45
Save men from death, and kill Corruption :
And many years ago the deed was done;
      His heart was pierc'd ; out of His side there ran
      Sinne's corrasives,[78] restoratives for man.

This precious balm I begg'd, for pitie's sake,   50
At Mercie's gate, where Faith alone may take
    What Grace and Truth do offer lib'rally.
Bounty said, 'Come.'   I heard it, and believ'd ;
None ever there complain'd but was reliev'd.

Hope waiting upon Faith said instantly,   55
That thenceforth I should live, Corruption dye.

And so she dy'd, I live. But yet, alas,
We are not parted : she is where she was,
    Cleaves fast unto me still, looks thro' mine eyes,
Speaks in my tongue, and museth in my mind;   60
Works with mine hands ; her body's left behind,
    Although her soul be gone.   My miseries   •
    All flow from hence; from hence my woes arise.

I loath myself, because I leave her not,
Yet cannot leave her.   No, she is my lot,   65
    Now being dead, that living was my choice;
And still, though dead, she both conceives and bears
Many faults daily, and as many fears :
    All which for vengeance call with a loud voice,
    And drown my comforts with their deadly noise. 70

Dead bodies kept unbury'd quickly stink
And putrifie: how can I, then, but think
    Corruption noysome, even mortifi'd ?[79]
Though such she were before, yet such to me
She seemèd not.   Kind fools can never see,   75
    Or will not credit, until they have try'd,
    That friendly looks oft false intents do hide.

But mortifi'd Corruption lies unmaskt,
Blabs her own secret filthiness unaskt,

To all that understand her : that do none   80
In whom she lives embracèd with delight :
She first of all deprives them of their sight;
    Then doat they on her, as upon their own,
    And she to them seems beautiful alone.⁸⁰

But woe is me !   One part of me is dead ;   85
    The other lives : yet that which lives is led,
  • Or rather carry'd, captive unto sin
By the dead part.   I am a living grave,
And a dead body I within me have.
    The worse part of the better oft doth win ;   90
    And when I should have ended, I begin.

The scent would choak me, were it not that Grace
Sometimes vouchsafeth to perfume the place
    With odours of the Spirit ; which do ease me,
And counterpoise Corruption.   Blessèd Spirit,   95
Although eternal torments be my merit,   =desert
    And of myself transgressions only please me,
    Adde grace enough, being reviv'd, to raise me.

Challenge Thine own ; let not intruders hold
Against Thy right what to my wrong I sold.   100
    Having no state myself, but tenancy,
And tenancy at will, what could I grant
That is not voided, if Thou say, Avaunt !   =annulled
    O speak the word, and make these inmates flee ;
    Or, which is one, take me to dwell with Thee. 105

44. THE CURB.

Peace, rebel thought; dost thou not know thy King,
　　　My God, is here?
Cannot His presence, if no other thing,
　　　Make thee forbear?
Or were He absent, all the standers-by　　　　　5
　　　Are but His spyes:
And well He knows, if thou shouldst it deny,
　　　Thy words were lyes.
If others will not, yet I must and will
　　　Myself complain.　　　　　10

My God, ev'n now a base rebellious thought
　　　Began to move,
And subt'ly twining with me would have wrought
　　　Me from Thy love:
Fain he would have me to believe that sin　　　15
　　　And Thou might both
Take up my heart together for your inne,
　　　And neither loath
The other's company; a while sit still,
　　　And part again.　　　　　20

Tell me, my God, how this may be redrest:
　　　The fault is great,
And I, the guilty party,[81] have confest
　　　I must be beat.
And I refuse not punishment for this,　　　　25

Though to my pain,
So I may learn to do no more amiss,
Nor sin again :
Correct me, if Thou wilt ; but teach me then
What I shall do.   30

Lord of my life, methinks I heard Thee say,
That labour's eas'd ;
The fault that is confesst is done away,
And Thou art pleas'd.
How can I sin again, and wrong Thee then,   35
That dost relent,
And cease Thine anger straight, as soon as men
Do but repent ?
No, rebel thought ; for if thou move again,
I'll tell that too.   40

45. THE LOSS.

The match[82] is made
Between my Love and me ;
And therefore glad
And merry now I'll be.
Come, glory, crown   5
My head ;
And, pleasures, drown
My bed
Of thorns in down.
Sorrow, be gone ;   10

Delight
    And joy alone
Befit
    My honeymoon.
Be packing now,   15
    You comb'rous cares and fears;
Mirth will allow
    No room to sighs and tears.
Whilst thus I lay,
    As ravisht with delight,   20
I heard one say,
    'So fools their friends requite.'
I knew the voice
    My Lord's;
        And at the noise   25
    His words
        Did make, arose.
I look'd and spy'd
    Each where,
        And loudly cry'd,   30
    'My dear;'
        But none reply'd.
Then to my grief
    I found my Love was gone,
Without relief,   35
    Leaving me all alone.[83]

46. THE SEARCH.

Whither, Oh ! whither is my Lord departed?
What, can my Love, that is so tender-hearted,
Forsake the soul which once He thorow darted,
          As if it never smarted ?

No, sure my Love is here, if I could find Him ;   5
He that fills all can leave no place behind Him.
But Oh ! my senses are too weak to wind[84] Him ;
          Or else I do not mind Him.

O no, I mind Him not so as I ought ;
Nor seek Him so as I by Him was sought,   10
When I had lost myself ; He dearly bought
          Me, that was sold for nought.

But I have wounded Him that made me sound ;
Lost Him again by Whom I first was found ;
Him that exalted me, have cast to th' ground ;   15
          My sins His bloud have drown'd.

Tell me, Oh! tell me—Thou alone canst tell—
Lord of my life, where Thou art gone to dwell ;
For in Thine absence heav'n itself is hell ;
          Without Thee none is well.   20

Or, if Thou beest not gone, but only hidest
Thy presence in the place where Thou abidest,
Teach me the sacred art which Thou providest
          For all them whom Thou guidest,

To seek and find Thee by : else here I'll lie,   25
Untill Thou find me. If Thou let me dye,
That only unto Thee for life do cry,
        Thou dy'st as well as I.

For if Thou live in me, and I in Thee,
Then either both alive or dead must be ;   30
At least I'll lay my death on Thee, and see
        If Thou wilt not agree.

For though Thou be the Judge Thyself, I have
Thy promise for it, which Thou canst not wave,
That who salvation at Thine hands do crave,   35
        Thou wilt not fail to save.

Oh! seek and find me, then ; or else deny
Thy truth, Thyself. Oh! Thou that canst not lye,
Show Thyself constant to Thy word, draw nigh ;
        Find me. Loe, here I lye.   40

47. THE RETURN.

    Loe, now my Love appears;
        My tears
    Have clear'd mine eyes ; I see
        'Tis He.
Thanks, blessèd Lord ; Thine absence was my hell ; 5
And now Thou art returnèd, I am well.

    By this I see I must
        Not trust

My joys unto myself;
This shelf[85]　　　　　　　　=reef 10
Of too secure and too presumptuous pleasure
Had almost sunk my ship and drown'd my treasure.

　　Who would have thought a joy
　　　　So coy,
　　To be offended so,　　　　　　15
　　　　And go
So suddenly away?　As if enjoying
Full pleasure and contentment were annoying,

　　Hereafter I had need
　　　　Take heed.　　　　　　20
　　Joyes, amongst other things,
　　　　Have wings,
And watch their opportunities of flight,
Converting in a moment day to night.

　　But is't enough for me　　　　25
　　　　To be
　　Instructed to be wise?
　　　　I'll rise,
And read a lecture unto them that are
Willing to learn, how comfort dwells with care.　　30

　　He that his joyes would keep
　　　　Must weep;
　　And in the brine of tears
　　　　And fears

Must pickle them. That powder[86] will preserve; 35
Faith with repentance is the soul's conserve.

       Learn to make much of care;
         A rare
      And precious balsom 'tis
        For bliss; 40
Which oft resides where mirth with sorrow meets;
Heavenly joys on earth are bitter-sweets.[87]

48. INUNDATIONS.

We talk of Noah's flood as of a wonder;
       And well we may;
       The Scriptures say
The water did prevail, the hills were under,
    And nothing could be seen but sea. 5

And yet there are two other floods surpass
       That flood as far
      As heav'n one star;
Which many men regard as little as
    The ordinari'st things that are. 10

The one is sin, the other is salvation;
       And we must need
      Confess indeed
That either of them is an inundation,
    Which doth the deluge far exceed. 15

In Noah's flood he and his houshold liv'd;
     And there abode
     A whole ark-load
Of other creatures that were then repriev'd;
    All safely on the waters rode.   20

But when sin came, it overflowèd all,
     And left none free;
     Nay, even He,
That knew no sin, could not release my thrall
    But that He was made sin for me;   25

And when salvation came, my Saviour's blood
     Drown'd sin again,
     With all its train
Of evils; overflowing them with good,
    With good that ever shall remain.   30

O let there be one other inundation;
     Let grace o'rflow
     In my soul so,
That thankfulness may level with salvation, =run level
    And sorrow sin may overgrow!   35

Then will I praise my Lord and Saviour so,
     That angels shall
     Admire man's fall,
When they shall see God's greatest glory grow,
    Where Satan thought to root out all.   40

49. SIN.

Sin, I would fain define thee, but thou art
    An uncouth thing;
    All that I bring
To show thee fully shows thee but in part.

I call thee ' the transgression of the law;'   5
    And yet I read
    That sin is dead
Without the law, and thence its strength doth draw.

I say thou art ' the sting of death.' 'Tis true ;
      And yet I find   10
      Death comes behind ;
The work is done before the pay be due.[88]

I say thou art the devil's work ; yet he
    Should much rather
    Call thee father ;   15
For he had been no devil but for thee.

What shall I call thee, then ? If death and devil,
    Right understood,
    Be names too good,
I'll say thou art the quintessence of evil.   20

50. TRAVELS AT HOME.

Oft have I wish'd a traveller to be ;   .
Mine eyes did even itch the sights to see
That I had heard and read of; oft I have
Been greedy of occasion as the grave,

That never saics 'enough ;' yet still was crost,   5
When opportunities had promis'd most.
At last I said, 'What mean'st thou, wandring elf,
To straggle thus ?   Go, travel first thyself.[89]
Thy little world can show thee wonders great ;
The greater may have more, but not more neat[90]   10
And curious pieces.   Search, and thou shalt find
Enough to talk of.   If thou wilt, thy mind
Europe supplies, and Asia thy will,
And Africk thine affections.   And if still
Thou list to travel further, put thy senses   15
For both the Indies.   Make no more pretences
Of new discoveries, whilst yet thine own
And nearest little world is still unknown.
Away, then, with thy quadrants, compasses,
Globes, tables, cards[91] and maps, and minute-glasses;   20
Lay by thy journals and thy diaries,
Close up thine annals and thine histories :
Study thyself, and read what thou hast writ
In thine own book, thy conscience.   Is it fit
To labour after other knowledge so,   25
And thine own nearest, dearest self not know?
Travels abroad both dear and dang'rous are,
Whilst oft the soul payes for the bodie's fare ;
Travels at home are cheap and safe : salvation
Comes mounted on the wings of meditation.   30
     He that doth live at home, and learns to know
     God and himself, needeth no further go.'

51. THE JOURNEY.

Life is a journey.   From our mothers' wombs,
As houses, we set out; and in our tombs,
As inns, we rest, till it be time to rise.
'Twixt rocks and gulfs our narrow footpath lies;
Haughty presumption and hell-deep despair   5
Make our way dangerous, though seeming fair.
The world, with its inticements sleek and sly,
Slabbers[92] our steps, and makes them slippery.
The flesh, with its corruptions, clogs our feet,
And burdens us with loads of lusts unmeet.   10
The devil where we tread doth spread his snares,
And with temptations takes us unawares.
Our footsteps are our thoughts, our words, our works;
These carry us along; in these there lurks
Envy, lust, avarice, ambition,   15
The crooked turnings to perdition.
One while we creep amongst the thorny brakes
Of worldly profits; and the devil takes
Delight to see us pierce ourselves with sorrow
To-day, by thinking what may be to-morrow.   20
Another while we wade and wallow in
Puddles of pleasure; and we never lin   =cease
Daubing ourselves with dirty damn'd delights,
Till self-begotten pain our pleasure frights.
Sometimes we scramble to get up the banks   25
Of icy honour; and we break our ranks

G

To step before our fellows; though they say,
He soonest tyreth that still leads the way.
Sometimes, when others justle and provoke us,
We stir that dust ourselves that serves to choak us ;   30
And raise those tempests of contention which
Blow us beside the way into the ditch.
Our minds should be our guids; but they are blind :
Our wills outrun our wits, or lag behind.
Our furious passions, like unbridled jades,   35
Hurry us headlong to th' infernal shades.
     If God be not our guide, our guard, our friend,
     Eternal death will be our journey's end.

52   ENGINES.

Men often find, when Nature's at a stand,
And hath in vain try'd all her utmost strength,
That Art, her ape, can reach her out an hand,
To piece her powers with to a full length :
     And may not Grace have means enough in store 5
     Wherewith to do as much as that, and more ?

She may : she hath engines of ev'ry kind
To work, what Art and Nature, when they view,
Stupendious[93] miracles of wonder find,
And yet must needs acknowledge to be true;   10
     So far transcending all their pow'r and might,
     That they stand ev'n amazèd at the sight.

Take but three instances ; faith, hope, and love.
Souls help'd by the perspective-glass of faith
Are able to perceive what is above   15
The reach of reason ; yea, the Scripture saith
    Ev'n Him that is invisible behold,
    And future things, as if they'd been of old.

Faith looks into the secret cabinet
Of God's eternal counsels, and doth see   20
Such mysteries of glory there as set
Believing hearts on longing ; till they be
    Transform'd to the same image, and appear
    So alterèd, as if themselves were there.

Faith can raise earth to heaven, or draw down   25
Heaven to earth, make both extreams to meet,—
Felicity and misery ; can crown
Reproach with honour, season sowre with sweet.
    Nothing's impossible to faith ; a man
    May do all things that he believes he can.   30

Hope founded upon faith can raise the heart
Above itself in expectation
Of what the soul desireth for its part ;
Then, when its time of transmigration
    Is delay'd longest, yet as patiently   35
    To wait, as if 'twere answer'd by and by.

When grief unwieldy grows, hope can abate
The bulk to what proportion it will ;

So that a large circumference of late
A little center shall not reach to fill ;   40
　　Nor that which gyant-like before did strout   strut
　　Be able with a pigmey's pace t' hold out.

Hope can disperse the thickest clouds of night
That fear hath overspread the soul withall ;
And make the darkest shadows shine as bright   45
As the sunbeams spread on a silver wall ;
　　Sin-shaken souls Hope, anchor-like, holds steady,
　　When storm and tempests make them more than
　　　　giddy.

Love led by Faith, and fed with Hope, is able
To travel through the world's wide wilderness ;   50
And burdens seeming most intollerable
Both to take up and bear with cheerfulness ;
　　To do or suffer what appears in sight
　　Extreamly heavy, Love will make most light.

Yea, what by men is done or suffered,   '   55
Either for God, or else for one another,
Though in itself it be much blemishèd
With many imperfections, which smother
　　And drown the worth and weight of it ; yet, fall
　　What will or can, Love makes amends for all.   60

Love doth unite and knit ; both make and keep
Things one together which were otherwise,

Or would be both divers and distant. Deep,
High, long, and broad, or whatsoever size
    Eternity is of, or happiness,   65
    Love comprehends it all, bee't more or less.

Give me this threefold cord of graces then,
Faith, Hope, and Love ; let them possess mine heart ; ·
And gladly I'll resign to other men
All I can claim by Nature or by Art: 70
    To mount[94] a soul, and make it still stand stable,
    These are alone engines incomparable.

TO MY REVEREND FRIEND THE AUTHOR OF THE SYNAGOGUE.

Sir,

I lov'd you for your Synagogue before
I knew your person ; but now love you more ;
    Because I find
It is so true a picture of your mind ;
        Which tunes your sacred lyre
        To that eternal quire,
        Where holy Herbert sits
        (O shame to prophane wits !)
And sings his and your anthems, to the praise
Of Him that is the First and Last of daies.

These holy hymns had an ethereal birth ;
For they can raise sad souls above the earth,
    And fix them there,
Free from the world's anxieties and fear.
        Herbert and you have pow'r
        To do this ; ev'ry hour
        I read you, kills a sin
        Or lets a virtue in
To fight against it ; and the Holy Ghost
Supports my frailties, lest the day be lost.

This holy war, taught by your happy pen,
The Prince of Peace approves.   When we poor men
           Neglect our arms,
W' are circumvested with a world of harms.
           But I will watch and ward,
           And stand upon my guard;
           And still consult with you
           And Herbert, and renew
My vows and say, ' Well fare his and your heart,
The fountains of such sacred wit and art.'

Iz[AAK] WA[LTON].

TO HIS INGENIOUS FRIEND

THE AUTHOR OF THE SYNAGOGUE,

UPON HIS ADDITIONAL CHURCH-UTENSILS.

    Sir,
    So the cheap touchstone's bold
    To question the more noble gold;
    As I, at your command,
    Put forth my blushing hand
To try these raptures, sent to my poor test;
But since your question's, ' Are they like the rest?'
    I say they are the best;
That once conceiv'd, the other is confest.

    But, sir, now they are here,
For to prevent a female jeer,
    Thus much affirm I do,
    They'r like the father too;

And you like him whose sublime paths you tread,
Herbert! to be like whom who'd not be dead?
        Herbert! whom when I read,
I stoop at stars that shine below my head.

        Herbert! whose every strain
Twists holy breasts with happy brain;
        So that who strives to be
        As elegant as he
Must climbe Mount Calv'ry for Parnassus' hill,
And in his Saviour's sides baptise his quill;
        A Jordan[95] fit t' instill
A saint-like stile, backt with an angel's skill.

        He was our Solomon,
And you are our Centurion;
        Our Temple him we owe,
        Our Synagogue to you;
Where, if your piety so much allow
That structure with these ornaments t' endow,
        All good men will avow
Your Syn'gogue, built before, is furnisht now.
                                        I. L.

    Sir,
While I read your lines, methinks I spie
Churches, and churchmen, and the old hierarchie:
What potent charms are these! you have the knack
To make men young again, and fetch time back.

I've lost what was bestow'd on Judah's prince,[96]
And am now where I was thrice five years since.
The mid-space shrunk to nothing; manners, men,
And times, and all look just as they did then;
Rubbish and ruin's vanisht, everywhere
Order and comliness afresh appear.
What cannot poets do? They change with ease
The face of things, and lead us as they please.
Yet here's no fiction neither: we may see
The poet, prophet; his verse, historie.   A. S.

    Jan. 1, 1654.

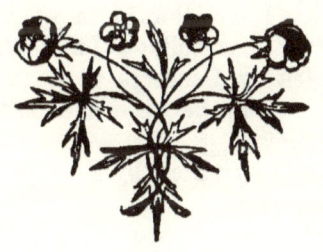

NOTES AND ILLUSTRATIONS.

[1] p. 5, ' *Subterliminare.*' In a contemporary handwriting I have ' Mr. Henry Vaughan' (=Henry Vaughan the Silurist) placed under the heading of Langford's lines ' To the Author' (on verso, of 5th edition of ' The Synagogue,' 1667) ; and in the same copy ' *Subterliminare*' is inscribed ' by Dr. Donne.' See our Memorial-Introduction on this.

[2] p. 6, ' *thwart*'=contradict.

[3] p. 9, ' *in tail :*' English law term=holding which is opposite to fee simple.

[4] p. 10, ' *fast*'=fasten.

[5] p. 10, ' *hood-winckt*'=blinded—from the hawking term.

[6] p. 10, ' *alchimy :*' the allusion is not to transmutation, but alchemy as chemistry, or rather chemistry applied to art.

[7] p. 10, ' *tincture :*' see Glossarial Index to HERBERT, vol. ii.

[8] p. 11, ' *Spirit's*'=the Holy Spirit. From the outset onward it has been misprinted ' spirits.' It might indeed be that there was a sort of verbal conceit or pun on ' spirits' and *aqua regia*, the ' spirits' so called ; for nitro-muriatic acid was called ' spirits,' just as sulphuric acid was ' spirits of vitriol.' But the primary and surely intended sense is that the gilded brass of hypocrisy passes as gold till detected as false by the test of the Holy Spirit. See 'Schola Cordis,' Ode xvi. line 47, and relative note.

[9] p. 11, ' *heardest last :*' that is, in 8. The Church.

[10] p 12, ' *solidate*'=consolidate (cf. solder).

[11] p. 15, ' *complement :*' seems to be used simply as an addition, and as somewhat between the exact sense of complement and our compliment.

[12] p. 15, ' *fœderal*'=granted by a perpetual treaty to him and his posterity for ever.

[13] p. 15, ' *Reading-pue :*' see Memorial - Introduction to HERBERT on the equal height of the pulpit and reading-desk at Leighton Bromswold; and in 4to (vol. i., facing page xxv.) a view of them.

¹⁴ p. 16, '*But* .... *alone.*' As though they were the only touchstones, &c. Rather a forced use of 'but.' The construction may be taken to be 'to their own [they bring], but alone [*i.e.* the only] touchstones,' &c.

¹⁵ p. 17, '*top*'=over-top. 'And topping all others in boasting' ('Coriolanus,' ii. 1).

¹⁶ p. 18, '*bears the bell:*' see Glossarial Index to HERBERT, vol. ii. *s v.*

¹⁷ p. 19, '*panchreston*'=all good, all-heal.

¹⁸ p. 19, '*perspective:*' see Glossarial Index to HERBERT, vol. ii. *s.v.*

¹⁹ p. 20, '*speaketh by this Book*'=the saying, 'he speaks by the book,' *i.e.* correctly, with exactness.

²⁰ p. 21, '*good cook.*' The old proverb, 'God sends the meat and the devil the cooks,' has a solemn meaning in it.

²¹ p. 23, '*toothsome*'=relishable, sweet.

²² p. 24, '*last course and best provision:*' a reminiscence of the saying of the governor of the feast at the marriage of Cana in Galilee.

²³ p. 24, '*tuch*'=basanites, or hard black granite; but sometimes used, says Nares, for any costly marble. See our edition of Sir PHILIP SIDNEY, vol. i. pp. 9, 12, 109, 112. Coleridge is in error in his note here : '*tuch* rhyming to *much*, from the German *tuch*, cloth. I never met with it before as an English word. So I find *platt* for foliage in Stanley's History of Philosophy.'

²⁴ p. 25, '*close*'=shut up, enclosed with rails; opposed to 'open,' as 'fixt' is to 'movable.'

²⁵ p. 25, '*So that*'=I will not take offence within these limits, namely, provided I be not driven to thwart authority; or to make a party for faction, *i.e.* for factious purposes, or be made the tool of a faction; and thirdly, provided I be not made even seemingly to make or join such a party. With such I must, in the interests both of unity and charity, take offence, or become their opponent.

²⁶ p. 26, '*dead:*' the addition of spirits of pearls would not vivify such wine, would not increase its flavour and other qualities, but 'deaden' it.

²⁷ p. 27, '*vail*'=lower, a nautical term for lowering the topsail, &c., as a sign of submission or compliment; and often applied in those days to the taking off and consequent lowering sweep of the bonnet or hat. See our DONNE, *s.v.*

[28] p. 28, '*vessel'd :*' Bacon uses this verb (Richardson, *s.v.*), but it is unusual. 'Invesselled' occurs in Mary Magdalene's Tears, st. 4. Both forms seem rare.

[29] p. 29, '*the many*'=the mob: 'Odi profanum vulgus et arceo' (Horace).

[30] p. 29, '*beesome*'=besom or broom.

[31] p. 30, '*tune*'=gives the note for and leads. So in 20. The Clerk, line 4.

[32] p. 31, '*most* . . . . *sanctifi'd*'=chiefly expecteth to be made, *i.e.* declared or praised as holy, '*sanctified*' being used in similar sense to '*glorified.*'

[33] p. 31, '*smells.*' He was probably thinking of mace, the envelope of the nutmeg.

[34] p. 32, '*poor :*' cf. St. Luke iv. 18 ; St. Matthew xix. 21 ; St. John xii. 5, 6.

[35] p. 34, '*countercharme*'=counter-spell, as in witchcraft.

[36] p. 35, '*chymick blessing.*' The phrase is rather oddly worded, but means is a curse transformed into a blessing. The cases were not alike ; but the thought was suggested by remembrance of Balaam and the wars of Amalek, and perhaps of the commanded Canaanitish vows. We cannot, he says, expect to obtain a blessing like reformation of religion in our own way, namely, by the curse of war, except—and that is rarely—when the over-ruling and transforming providence of God chooses to turn it into a blessing.

[37] p. 36, '*gen'rally*'=in the general sense of the word, according to its etymology.

[38] p. 37, '*proceed*'=advance or seek to occupy higher office.

[39] p. 38, '*ready prest :*' somewhat tautological, but emphatic=readily, ready, or ready-hasted. Fr. prêt, prest ; Latin, præstare. In sense and etymology the word is different from prest or pressed of verb 'to press.'

[40] p. 39, '*censures*'=judgments, decisions.

[41] p. 39, '*attone :*' according to its etymology to at-one, to make at one.

[42] p. 40, ' An instance of *proving too much*' (Coleridge).

[43] p. 41, '*persons :*' ' Functions of times, but not persons of necessity ? Ex. bishop to archbishop' (Coleridge).

[44] p. 43, '*florilegia :*' a common name for collections of sentences from the Fathers, &c.

[45] p. 43, ' *That he loves God,*' &c. ' Equally unthinking and uncharitable. I approve of them ; but yet remember Roman

Catholic idolatry, and that it originated in such high-flown metaphors as these' (Coleridge).

⁴⁶ p. 43, *The Sabbath, or Lord's Day.* 'Make it sense and lose the rhyme; or make it rhyme and lose the sense' (Coleridge).

⁴⁷ p. 44, ' *blazon*'=emblazon.

⁴⁸ p. 45, '*consort :*' see our HERBERT's Glossarial Index, vol. ii. *s.v.*

⁴⁹ p. 45, ' *t' amuse*'=make muse.

⁵⁰ p. 46, *The Nativity :* see our Memorial-Introduction for Coleridge on this poem.

⁵¹ p. 46, '*Shine forth, bright sun:*' 'Shine out, fair sun' (' Richard III.' i. 2).

⁵² p. 47, ' *that we could*'=this day, in order that we might, &c., the intermediate clause being parenthetical.

⁵³ p. 48, ' *copy.*' The meaning, as not unfrequently, is the original which supplied the copies, just as the schoolboy's ' copy' is that set for him to copy.

⁵⁴ p. 49, ' *but we*'=but of what we were or are.

⁵⁵ p. 49, ' *livelihood*'=lifeship, state of life.

⁵⁶ p. 49, ' *water's bloud.*' Holding circumcision and baptism as the sacraments of admission into the old and new Covenants respectively, he had come therefrom to the thought expressed in the lines from ' Original Sin' onwards, that the circumcision of Christ was not the putting off of the body of His sins, but the entering of Himself as man in the covenant between God and corrupt man, like as in baptism we are admitted to partake of Christ's righteousness. Now he goes farther, and expresses more fully the oneness of Christ with the believer, and of the believer with Christ, through the inter-communion, as it were, of His circumcision and our baptism. Christ having entered Himself as man, and made Himself one in all things with us, it was thus His blood gave its virtues to our baptism, and made it a baptism by which we are baptised into His circumcision and purity—' in Whom also ye are circumcised with the circumcision made without hands, in putting off the body of the sins of the flesh by the circumcision of Christ' (Col. ii. 11; with which also Harvey probably connected 1 St. John i. 7, Hebrews ix. 22, and the like).

⁵⁷ p. 49, ' *quit*'=quite, requite, give in equal exchange.

⁵⁸ p. 49, Romans ii. 29. Same signification Romans vi. 3, 4 ; Col. ii. 11, 12 ; Gal. iii. 27.

[59] p. 52, '*If I do not:*' I am glad I am in such a frame of mind that I would grieve, were it not that I rather joy in the exceeding love thus manifested for me.

[60] p. 54, '*sin-seisĕd:*' a technical legal term for taking possession.

[61] p. 55, '*tour*'=tower, *i.e.* rise straight aloft as a hawk, lark, and sometimes other birds.

[62] p. 56, '*shaken.*' 'The spiritual miracle was the descent of the Holy Ghost—the outward, the wind, and the tongues; and so St. Peter himself explains it. That each individual obtained the power of speaking all languages is neither contained in, nor fairly deducible from, St. Luke's account' (Coleridge).

[63] p. 57, '*earnest*'=first payment or deposit.

[64] p. 57, '*legier:*' or ledger ambassador, same as resident ambassador. See Glossarial Index to HERBERT, vol. ii. *s.v.*

[65] p. 59, '*transcend:*' 'Most true, but not *contradict*. Reason is to faith as the eye to the telescope' (Coleridge).

[66] p. 59, '*in gross:*' in bulk or in wholesale quantities, the gross being a number which measured wholesale quantities, besides otherwise lending itself to the idea of large quantity. See 'Schola Cordis,' Ode ix. line 19, and relative note.

[67] p. 59, '*lift*'=lift or lifted; a shortened form of the past of verbs in *t*, occasionally used by Greene and others, but which appears to have become more common in the later part of the reign of James. A notable example occurs in the 'Tempest' (i. 2), where Prospero, speaking of their exposure at sea, says of the 'carcass of a butt' [the hull of a Mediterranean vessel so called],

> 'the very rats
> Instinctively have [had] quit it : there they hoist us;'

where exception has been taken to Rowe's change 'had,' and to Shakespeare's supposed change from the past tense in the previous lines to the historical present, through inattention to the fact that 'quit' and 'hoist' are=quitted and hoisted.

[68] p. 62, '*beshrew:*' a slight maledictory exclamation=sorrow upon, a vexation or mischief on. This is on the supposition that it and a shrew and a shrew-mouse came directly from the Saxon. But Minsheu says that it came (intermediately) from the shrew or shrew-mouse; 'a *shrew* mouse, quasi shrewd [*i.e.* as he explains shrewd, ill] mouse, which, by biting cattell, so venometh them that they die ¶ Gesu: whereof came our English, "I beshrew thee," when we wish ill;' and he repeats, *s.v.v.*,

beshrew and mouse, where he also says and shows by the words that the shrew-mouse, being accounted venomous, was 'therefore called in divers languages his name as his nature is.' Even if we do not adopt this derivation, his authority may be taken as proving that the original sense was more maledictory than that given above, and that Sherwood was right in his English-French Cotgrave in translating beshrew by maudire. Other uses of shrew and shrewd tend to the same; but if originally more imprecatory, there can be no doubt that it became slighter and more innocent, partly perhaps from its likeness to shrew, a woman scold, partly from the after-adoption of more forcible and Low-Country swearing.

[69] p. 63, 'score'=Yet I am again run into debt. See Glossarial Index to HERBERT, vol. ii. s.v.

[70] p. 64, 'gravell'd:' now relegated to vulgar colloquial or slang, a metaphor=thrown on the ground or dust, and probably derived from wrestling.

[71] p. 64, 'lists .... snarled ruffs.' Snarl, of root snare, has a similar meaning to entangle, or substantive an entanglement, the le being, as usual, a frequentative or reduplicative form. I believe it was (perhaps is) used for certain specific twists or hanks of woollen thread, &c. Accordingly I have ventured to read 'knot-snarled' instead of 'knots snarled ruffs,' regarding the s as having been inadvertently reduplicated. 'Lists'=the selvedge portion of woollen cloth.

[72] p. 65, 'rammish'=tastes of an unpleasant rankness, or, to use a better equivalent, 'tastes goatish.'

[73] p. 65, 'wash and draff'=trash, waste-stuff (technical 'brewing' terms).

[74] p. 65, 'list=desire, choose.

[75] p. 66, 'be sorry'=When I shall sorrow for or after renown.

[76] p. 67, 'score'=chalk it on the score, go in debt: see note[63].

[77] p. 68, 'third.' Not twist both deaths into a third death, which is contrary to scriptural phraseology and ideas, and does not agree with the metaphorical words following; but twist them both into a third, which is an old form of 'thrid' or thread. Nares justly observes that we have the same word in

'For I
Have given you a third of my own life,
Or that for which I live.'

(Prospero giving Miranda to Ferdinand, 'Tempest,' iv. 1.) Though endeavours have been made to explain it as one-third, such explanations make the passage worse than nonsense by making it ridiculous.

[78] p. 68, '*sin's corrasives:*' 'corrosives' is=that eat into and destroy sin. But query is 'corra' not a press error?

[79] p. 69, '*mortified:*' a conceitfully used word: 'mortified' in the sense in which we use mortification of the flesh (after the phrase of St. Paul), and mortified, dead-struck.

[80] p. 70, '*alone:*' I have met somewhere with a weird Scottish ballad of a knight whose mother was burnt for a witch or for heresy, and who married a hag from abroad, beautiful to him and to him alone, till he had revenged his mother's death. The hag = murderous revenge.

[81] p. 71, '*party*'=individual (vulgarism now).

[82] p. 72, '*match*'=marriage or engagement.

[83] p. 73, may be said to be founded on the Song of Solomon.

[84] p. 74, '*wind:*' technical hunting term for to scent an animal of chase in the wind, so as to pursue on his traces and find him.

[85] p. 76, '*shelf*'=reef. See Glossarial Index to HERBERT, vol. ii. *s.v.*

[86] p. 77, '*powder:*' not strictly applicable to brine; but he was thinking of the salt added in powder to pickled meat, in order further to preserve it, and which, mingled with the exuded juices, becomes brine, at least in part.

[87] p. 77, '*bitter-sweets*'=the love-apple or fruit of *Solanum dulcamara*. So Vaux (?) of Beauty: 'Ah! bitter-sweet, infecting as the poison.'

[88] p. 79, '*be due:*' though sin be the sting of death, yet death comes behind, *i.e.* lagging behind, comes at some long time afterwards. The work is done by the deadly sting, but the due of it, death, comes not immediately, but long after. The conceit lies in the sting being spoken of as the sting of death, as we would of the bite of a serpent; yet the sting and the death are separate, and separate by some interval of time.

[89] p. 80, '*travel first thyself*'=go travel first over thyself. The little world or microcosm was a favourite phrase and thought, because it was held that man was a little world, having analogies and relationships and sympathies, each part with each part of the greater world, the earth and its products. This thought was the basis of Fletcher's 'The Purple Island.'

[90] p. 80, '*neat:*' here=dainty, nice.

[91] p. 80, '*cards:*' used in those days both for charts and

the mariner's compass, *i.e.* the card of the compass. Here it is used for the latter, as shown by the word ' maps' and ' compasses ;' above, as shown by ' quadrants,' is the mathematical instrument so called. See our edition of SOUTHWELL, pp. 44-5.

⁹² p. 81, ' *Slabbers :*' much the same as slobbers. Minsheu says 'slabber, to slubber or sully, *v.* to foule;' but here, as slab is a smooth flat stone, &c., so slabber is to make smooth with any fluid, just as grease is to make smooth and slippery with grease.

⁹³ p. 82, ' *stupendious :*' a spelling found much later, as in Marvell.

⁹⁴ p. 85, ' *mount*'=raise.

⁹⁵ p. 88, ' *a Jordan :*' see HERBERT's Glossarial Index, vol. ii. *s. v.*=vol. i. pp. 63, 283. I take this further opportunity of remarking with reference to Herbert's headings of ' Jordan,' that in 75. Jordan the meaning is—When he first joyed in the Lord he sought out best means to express that joy; but that now, when he had crossed over for good and become a settled inhabitant of God's promised land, all he need do is to speak in simple words what love dictates. In this he imitates somewhat the thought in Sidney's first sonnet (Astrophel and Stella). On another occasion he says, that in the fulness of its joy his heart can only repeat, ' My Joy, my Life, my Crown,' but that this is ' a true hymn' (131). In 25. Jordan the thought is similar=. Now having once for all crossed Jordan, my joy can only express itself simply, and what more is required when a loving heart would speak the truth ? Is there no beauty in Truth herself ? Can she need adornment ? Do I require to embellish my verse with those inventions and ornaments which poets find necessary when describing and praising either their mistresses adorned by art or the fictions of their own minds ? No ; in my great happiness I can but say, ' My God, my King ;' but it is my heart verse, it has the beauty of truth, and is so accepted of the God of all truth. In 75. he says that a true loving heart needs only to express itself simply as it feels ; in the other two, that in his fulness of joy he can but speak brokenly, but that such words are true songs, and having the beauty of truth, require not the adornment of a laboured wit. Harvey follows here in Herbert's footsteps.

⁹⁶ p. 89, ' *I've lost what was bestowed on Judah's prince.*' A reference to the fifteen years added to the life of Hezekiah (2 Kings xx. 1-6).   G.

H

II.

SCHOLA CORDIS.

Opposite is the title-page of the only edition of 'Schola Cordis' published during the author's lifetime, and which is our text. See our Preface and Memorial-Introduction for notices of other editions, and of the Emblems and for their source.

G.

Schola Cordis

or

The Heart of it Selfe,

gone away from God ;

brought back againe to him ;

& instructed by him.

Audiam quid
Loquatur in me
Dominus.
Psalm 84.

in 47

Emblems.

Loquar ad
Cor. Osa. 2.

London
Printed for H Blunden at the
Castle in Corn-hill 1647
Michael   van Iochem fecit
[12mo.]

To the Divine Majestie

of the onely begotten, eternall,
well-beloved Son of God and
Saviour of the world, *Christ Jesus*,
the King of Kings and Lord of Lords,
the Maker, the Mender, the Searcher, and the Teacher of
the Heart ;

The meanest of his most unworthy Servants offers up this poore account of his Thoughts, humbly begging pardon for all that is amisse
in them, and a gracious acceptance
of these weak Endeavours for
the advancement of His
Honor in the good
of others.

THE CONTENTS.

THE SCHOOL OF THE HEART.

THE INTRODVCTION.

TURNE in, my mind, wander no more abroad;
Here's[1] work enough at home,[2] lay by that load
Of scatter'd thoughts, that clogs and cumbers thee:
Resume thy long-neglected liberty
Of selfe-examination; bend thine eye   5
Inward, consider where thine heart doth lie,
How 'tis affected, how 'tis busi'd: looke
What thou hast writ thy selfe in thine own booke,
Thy conscience; here set thou thy selfe to schoole.
Selfe-knowledge, 'twixt a wise man and a foole   1o
Doth make the difference; he that neglects
This learning, sideth with his owne defects.
Dost thou draw backe? Hath custome charm'd thee so,
That thou canst relish nothing but thy woe?
Findst thou such sweetnesse in those sugar'd[3] lyes?   15
Have forain objects so ingrost thine eyes?
Canst thou not hold them off? Hast thou an care
To listen but to what thou shouldst not heare?
Art thou incapable of every thing
But what thy senses to thy fancie bring?   20

Remember that thy birth and constitution
Both promise better then such base confusion :
Thy birth's divine, from heaven ; thy composure[4]
Is spirit, and immortall ; thine inclosure
In walls of flesh, not to make thee debtor　　　25
For house-roome to them, but to make them better.
Thy body's thy freehold ; live, then, as the lord,
No tenant, to thine owne ; some time afford
To view what state 'tis in ; survey each part,
And above all take notice of thine heart :　　　30
Such as that is, the rest is or will be,
Better or worse, blame-worthy or fault-free.
What ! are the ruines such thou art affraid,
Or else asham'd to see how 'tis decai'd ?
Is 't therefore thou art loth to see it such　　　35
As now it is, because it is so much
Degenerated now from what it was
And should have been ?　Thine ignorance, alas,
Will make it nothing better, and the longer
Evils are suffer'd grow, they grow the stronger.　　40
Or hath thine understanding lost its light ?
Hath the darke night of error dimm'd thy sight,
So that thou canst not, though thou wouldst, observe
All things amisse within thee—how they swerve
From the straight rules of righteousnesse and reason ?　45
If so, omit not then this precious season :
Tis yet schoole-time, as yet the doore's not shut.
Harke how the Master calls ! Come, let us put

Up our requests to Him, Whose will alone
Limits His pow'r of teaching ; from Whom none   50
Returnes unlearnèd that hath once a will
To be His scholar, and implore His skill.
Great Searcher of the heart, Whose boundless sight
Discovers secrets, and doth bring to light
The hidden things of darkenesse ; Who alone   55
Perfectly knowst all things that can be knowne,—
Thou knowst I doe not, cannot, have no mind
To know mine heart ; I am not onely blind,
But lame and listlesse : Thou alone canst make
Mee able, willing ; and the paines I take,   60
As well as the successe, must come from Thee,
Who workest both to will and doe in mee :
Having now made mee willing to be taught,
Make mee as willing to learne what I ought.
Or, if Thou wilt allow Thy scholar leave   65
To choose his lesson,—lest I should deceive
My selfe againe, as I have done too often,—
Teach mee to know mine heart. Thou, Thou canst soften,
Lighten, enliven, purifie, restore,
And make more fruitfull then it was before   70
Its hardnesse, darkenesse, death, uncleannesse, losse,
And barrenesse ; refine it from the drosse,
And draw out all the dregs ; heal ev'ry sore ;
Teach it to know it selfe, and love Thee more.
    Lord, if Thou wilt, Thou canst impart this skill ;   75
    And for all other learning, take 't who will.[5]

1. THE INFECTION OF THE HEART.

Why hath Satan filled thine heart? Acts v. 3.

EPIGR. I.

Whilst thou enclin'st thy voyce-enveigled eare
The subtill serpent's syren-songs to heare;
Thy heart drinks deadly poyson drawn from hell,
And with a vip'rous brood of sinne doth swell.[6]

ODE I.

1. *The Soule.*

Profit and pleasure, comfort and content,
Wisedome and honour; and when these are spent,
A fresh supply of more.   Oh heav'nly words !
Are these the dainty fruits that this faire tree affords ?

2. *The Serpent.*

Yes, these and many more, if more may be ;   5
All that the world containes in this one tree
Contracted is.   Take but a tast, and try ;
Thou maist beleeve thy self, experience can not lye.

3. *The Soule.*

But thou must lye, and with a false pretence
Of friendship, rob me of that excellence   10
Which my Creator's bounty hath bestow'd
And freely given me, to whom He nothing ow'd.

4. *The Serpent.*

Strange composition ! so credulous,
And at the same time so suspicious !
This is the tree of knowledge, and untill   15
Thou eat thereof, how canst thou know what's good or ill?

5. *The Soule.*

God infinitly good my Maker is,
Who neither will nor can doe ought amisse ;
The being I receiv'd was that He sent,
And therefore I am sure must needs be excellent.   20

6. *The Serpent.*

Suppose it be ; yet doubtlesse He that gave
Thee such a being must Himselfe needs have
A better farre, more excellent by much ;
Or else be sure that He could not have made thee such.

7. *The Soule.*

Such as He made me I am well content   25
Still to continue ; for, if He had meant
I should enjoy a better state, He would
As easily as not have giv'n it, if He would.

8. *The Serpent.*

And is it not all one, if He have given
Thee meanes to get it ? must He still be driven   30
To new workes of creation for thy sake ?
Wilt thou not what He sets before thee daine to take ?

9. *The Soule.*

Yes, of the fruits of all the other trees
I freely take and eat ; they are the fees
Allow'd me for the dressing by the Maker ;   .35
But of this fatall fruit I must not be partaker.

10. *The Serpent.*

And why ? what danger can it be to eat
That which is good, being ordain'd for meat ?
What wilt thou say ? ' God made it not for food' ?
Or durst thou think that made by Him it is not good ? 40

11. *The Soule.*

Yes, good it is, no doubt, and good for meat ;
But I am not allow'd thereof to eat :
My Maker's prohibition, under paine
Of death the day I eat thereof, makes me refraine.

12. *The Serpent.*

Faint-hearted fondling, canst thou feare to dye,   45
Being a spirit and immortal ?   Fie !
God knowes this fruit, once eaten, will refine
Thy grosser parts alone, and make thee all divine.

13, 14. *The Soule.*

There's something in it, sure ; were it not good,
It had not in the midst of th' garden stood ;   50
And being good, I can no more refraine
From wishing then I can the fire to burne restraine.

Why doe I trifle, then ? what I desire
Why doe I not ? Nothing can quench the fire
Of longing but fruition. Come what will, 55
Eat it I must, that I may know what's good and ill.

15. *The Serpent.*

So thou art taken now ; that resolution
Gives an eternall date to thy confusion :
The knowledge thou hast got of good and ill
Is of good gone and past, of evill present still. 60

2. THE TAKING AWAY OF THE HEART.

Whoredome and wine and new wine take away the heart. Hosea iv. 11.

EPIGR. II.

Base lust and luxury, the scumme and drosse
Of hell-borne pleasures, please thee, to the losse
Of thy soul's precious eyesight, reason ; so
Mindlesse thy mind, heartlesse thine heart doth grow.

ODE II.

1. Laid downe already, and so fast asleepe ?
   Thy precious heart left loosly on thine hand,
   Which with all diligence thou shouldest keep,
   And guard against those enemies that stand
   Ready prepar'd to plunge it in the deep 5
   Of all distresse ? Rouse thee, and understand
       In time what in the end thou must confesse :
       That misery at last and wretchednesse
   Is all the fruit that springs from slothful idlenesse.

I

2. Whilst thou liest[7] soaking in security,   10
   Thou drownst thy selfe in sensuall delight,
   And wallowst in debauchèd luxurie;
   Which, when thou art awake and seest, will fright
   Thine heart with horror.   When thou shalt descry
   By the daylight the danger of the night,   15
       Then, then, if not too late, thou wilt confesse
       That endlesse misery and wretchednesse
   Is all the fruit that springs from riotous excesse.

3. Whilst thou dost pamper thy proud flesh, and thrust
   Into thy panch the prime of all thy store, =paunch 20
   Thou dost but gather fuell for that lust
   Which, boyling in thy liver,[8] runneth o're
   And frieth[9] in thy throbbing veines; which must
   Needs vent or burst when they can hold no more.
       But Oh, consider what thou shalt confesse   25
       At last, that misery and wretchednesse
   Is all the fruit that springs from lustfull wantonnesse.

4. Whilst thou dost feed effeminate desires
   With spumy[10] pleasures; whilst fruition
   The coals of lust fannes into flaming fires,   30
   And spurious delights thou doatest on,—
   Thy mind through cold remissnesse ev'n expires,
   And all the active vigour oft is gone.
       Take heed in time, or else thou shalt confesse
       At last that misery and wretchednesse   35
   Is all the fruit that springs from carelesse-mindednesse.

5. Whilst thy regardlesse sense-dissolvèd mind
Lies by unbent, that should have been thy spring
Of motion, all thy headstrong passions find
Themselves let loose, and follow their own swing, 40
Forgetful of the great account behind ;[11]
As though there never would be such a thing.
    But when it comes indeed, thou wilt confesse
    That misery alone and wretchednesse   44
Is all the fruit that springs from soule-forgetfulnesse.

6. Whilst thou remembrest not thy later end,
Nor what a reck'ning one day thou must make,
Putting no difference betwixt foe and friend,
Thou sufferst hellish fiends thine heart to take,
Who, all the while thou triflest, doe attend,   50
Ready to bring it to the burning lake
    Of fire and brimstone; where thou shalt confesse
    That endlesse misery and wretchednesse
Is all the fruit that springs from stupid heartlessnesse.

3. THE DARKENESSE OF THE HEART.

Their foolish heart was darkened.   Romans i. 21.

EPIGR. III.

Svch cloudy shadowes have eclips'd thine heart
As Nature cannot parallel, nor Art :
Vnlesse thou take My light of truth to guide thee,
Blacknesse of darknesse will at last betide thee.

ODE III.

1. Tarry, O tarry, lest thine heedlesse hast
Hurry thee headlong unto hell at last;
  See, see, thine heart's already half-way there;
Those gloomy shadowes that encompasse it
Are the vast confines of th' infernall pit.   5
    O stay, and if thou lov'st not light, yet feare
      That fatall darkenesse, where
      Such danger doth appeare.

2. A night of ignorance hath overspread
Thy mind and understanding; thou art led   10
  Blindfolded by unbridled passion;
Thou wandrest in the crooked ways of errour,
Leading directly to the King of Terrour:
    The course thou takest, if thou holdest on,
      Will bury thee anon   15
      In deep destruction.

3. Whilst thou art thus deprivèd of thy sight,
Thou knowst no difference betweene noone and night;
  Though the sun shine, yet thou regardst it not;
My love-alluring beauty cannot draw thee,   20
Nor doth my mind-amating[12] terrour awe thee:
    Like one that had both good and ill forgot,
      Thou carest not a jot
      What falleth to thy lot.

4. Thou art become unto thy selfe a stranger,   25
Observest not thine own desert or danger;

Thou knowst not what thou dost, nor canst thou
Whither thou goest : shooting in the darke,   [tel
How canst thou ever hope to hit the marke?
    What expectation hast thou to doe well?   30
      Thou art content to dwell
      Within the verge of hell.

5. Alas, thou hast not so much knowledge left
As to consider that thou art bereft   [though
    Of thine owne eyesight. But thou runnst as
Thou sawest all before thee; whilst thy minde   36
To neerest necessary things is blind.
    Thou knowest nothing as thou oughtst to know,
      Whilst thou esteemest so
      The things that are below.   40

6. Would ever any that had eyes mistake
As thou art wont to doe? no difference make
    Betwixt the way to heaven and to hell?
But, desperatly devoted to destruction,
Rebell against the light, abhorre instruction?   45
    As though thou didst desire with death to dwell,
      Thou hatest to heare tell
      How yet thou maist doe well.

7. O that thou didst but see how blind thou art,
And feel the dismall darknesse of thine heart!   50
    Then wouldst thou labour for, and I would lend,
My light to guide thee, that's not light alone,
But life, eyes, sight, grace, glory, all in one;

Then shouldst thou know whither those by-wayes
And that death in the end   [bend,
On darkenesse doth attend.   56

4. THE ABSENCE OF THE HEART.

Wherefore is there a price in the hand of a foole to get wisdome, seeing
he hath no heart to it? Proverbs xvii. 16.

EPIGR. IV.

Hadst thou an heart, thou fickle fugitive,
How would thine heart hate and disdaine to live
Mindfull of such vaine trifles as these be,
Resting forgetfull of itselfe and me!

ODE IV.

1. *The Soule.*

Brave, dainty, curious, rare, rich, precious things,
Able to make fate-blasted mortals blest;
Peculiar treasures and delights for kings,
That having pow'r of all would choose the best.
    How doe I hugge mine happinesse, that have   5
    Present possession of what others crave!

2. *Christ.*

Poore, silly, simple, sense-besotted soule,
Why dost thou hugge thy self-procurèd woes?
Release thy freeborne thoughts; at least controul
Those passions that enslave thee to thy foes.   10
    How wouldst thou hate thy self, if thou didst know
    The basenesse of those things thou prizest so!

3. *The Soule.*

They talk of goodnesse, vertue, piety,
Religion, honesty, I know not what;
So let them talk for me : so long as I   15
Have goods, and lands, and gold, and jewells, that
    Both equall and excell all other treasure,   [sure ?
    Why should I strive to make their paine my plea-

4. *Christ.*

So swine neglect the pearles that lie before them,
Trample them under foote, and feed on draffe :   20
So fooles gild rotten idols, and adore them ;
Cast all the corne away, and keep the chaffe.
    That ever reason should be blinded so,
    To graspe the shadow, let the substance goe !

5. *The Soule.*

All's but opinion that the world accounts   25
Matter of worth ; as this or that man sets
A value on it, so the price amounts ;
The sound of strings is varied by the frets.
    My mind's my kingdome; why should I withstand
    Or question that which I myselfe command ?   30

6. *Christ.*

Thy tyrant passions captivate thy reason ;
Thy lusts usurpe the guidance of the mind ;
Thy sense-led fancy barters good for geason ;[13]
Thy seed is vanity, thine harvest wind ;

Thy rules are crooked, and thou writ'st awry;   35
Thy wayes are wand'ring, and thine end to die.

7. *The Soule.*

This table summes me myriads of pleasure ;
That booke enroules mine honour's inventory;
These bags are stuft with millions of treasure;
Those writings evidence my state of glory;   40
    These bells ring heav'nly musicke in mine eares,
    To drown the noise of cumbrous cares and feares.

8, 9. *Christ.*

Those pleasures one day will procure thy paine ;
That which thou glori'st in will be thy shame;
Thou'lt finde thy losse in what thou thoughtst thy gaine;
Thine honour will put on another name;   46
    That musicke in the close will ring thy knell,
    Instead of heaven toll thee into hell.

But why doe I thus wast My words in vaine
On one that's wholly taken up with toyes;   50
That will not loose one dramme of earth to gaine =lose
A full eternall weight of heav'nly joyes ?
    All's to no purpose ; 'tis as good forbeare
    As speak to one that hath no heart to heare.

5. THE VANITY OF THE HEART.

Let not him that is deceived trust in vanity; for vanity shall be his
recompence. Job xv. 31.

EPIGR. V.

Ambition's bellowes, with the wind of honour,
Puffe up the swelling heart that dotes upon her;
Which, fill'd with empty vanity, breaths forth
Nothing but such things as are nothing worth.

ODE V.

1. The bane of kingdomes, world's disquieter,
   Hell's heire-apparent, Satan's eldest sonne,
   Abstract of ills, refinèd elixir,
   And quintessence of sinne—Ambition,
   Sprung from th' infernall shades, inhabits here, 5
   Making man's heart its horrid mansion;
       Which, though it were of vast content before,
       Is now puft up, and swells still more and
       more.

2. Whole armies of vaine thoughts it entertaines;
   Is stuft with dreames of kingdomes and of crownes;
   Presumes of profit without care or paines; 11
   Threatens to baffle all its foes with frownes;
   In ev'ry bargaine makes account of gaines;
   Fancies such frolicke mirth as choakes and drownes

The voyce of conscience; whose loud alarmes
Cannot be heard for Pleasure's counter-charmes.

3. Wer't not for anger and for pity, who
Could choose but smile to see vain-glorious men
Racking their wits, straining their sinewes so,
That thorow their transparent thinnesse, when   20
They mete with wind and sun, they quickly grow
Riv'led and dry, shrinke till they crack againe;
    And all but to seeme greater then they are;
    Stretching their strength, they lay their weak-
    nesse bare.   =wrinkled, l. 22

4. See how hell's fueller his bellowes plies,   25
Blowing the fire that burnt too fast before;
See how the furnace flames, the sparkles rise,
And spread themselves abroad still more and more;
See how the doating soule hath fixt her eyes
On her deare fooleries, and doth adore   30
    With hands and heart lift up, those trifling toyes
    Wherewith the devill cheates her of her joyes.

5. Alas, thou art deceiv'd; that glitt'ring crowne
On which thou gazest is not gold, but grief;
That scepter, sorrow: if thou take them downe,   35
And try them, thou shalt find what poore relief
They could afford thee, though they were thine owne;
Didst thou command ev'n all the world in chief,
    Thy comforts would abate, thy cares encrease,
    And thy perplexèd thoughts disturb thy peace.

6. Those pearles so thorow pierc'd, and strung together,
Though jewells in thine eyes they may appeare,
Will prove continu'd perills; when the weather
Is clouded once, which yet is faire and cleare,   44
What will that fanne, though of the finest feather,
Steed thee the brunt of windes and stormes to beare?
    Thy flagging colours hang their drooping head,
    And the shrill trumpet's sound shall strike thee
    dead.

7. Were all those balls which thou in sport dost tosse
Whole worlds, and in thy power to command,   50
The gaine would never countervaile all the losse;
Those slipp'ry globes will glide out of thine hand;
Thou canst have no fast hold but of the Crosse;
And thou wilt fall where thou dost thinke to stand.
    Forsake these follies, then, if thou wilt live: 55
    Timely repentance may thy death reprive.

6. THE OPPRESSION OF THE HEART.

Take heed lest at any time your hearts be overcharged with surfeiting and
drunkennesse. Lvke xxi. 34.

EPIGR. VI.

Two massy weights—surfeiting, drunkennesse—
Like mighty logs of lead, doe so oppresse
The heav'n-borne hearts of men, that to aspire
Vpwards they have nor power nor desire.

Ode VII.

1. Monster of sins ! see how th' inchanted soule
    O'rcharg'd already calls for more;
See how the hellish skinker[14] plies his bowle,
    And's ready furnishèd with store ;
      Whilst cups, on every side   5
      Planted, attend the tide.

2. See how the pilèd dishes mounted stand,
    Like hills advancèd upon hills ;
And the abundance both of sea and land
    Doth not suffice ev'n what it fills—   10
      Man's dropsy appetite,
      And cormorant delight.[15]

3. See how the poyson'd body's puft and swell'd ;
    The face enflamèd glowes with heat ;
The limbs unable are themselves to welld ;[16]   15
    The pulses Death's alarme doe beat :
      Yet man sits still and laughs,
      Whilst his owne bane he quaffes.

4. But where's thine heart the while, thou senselesse sot?
    Looke how it lieth crusht and quell'd ;   20
Flat beaten to the board, that it cannot
    Move from the place where it is held ;
      Nor upward once aspire
      With heavenly desire.

5. Thy belly is thy god, thy shame thy glory;   25
    Thou mindest only earthly things;
And all thy pleasure is but transitory,
    Which grief at last and sorrow brings:
        The courses thou dost take
        Will make thine heart to ake.   30

6. Is't not enough to spend thy precious time
    In empty idle complement;[17]
Unlesse thou straine (to aggravate thy crime)
    Nature beyond its owne extent,
        And force it to devoure   35
        An age within an houre?

7. That which thou swallowst is not lost alone,
    But quickly will revengèd be
By seasing on thine heart; which, like a stone,
    Lyes buri'd in the middst of thee,   40
        Both void of common sense
        And reason's excellence.

8. Thy body is disease's rendevouze;
    Thy mind the market-place[18] of vice;
The devill in thy will keeps open house;   45
    Thou liv'st as though thou wouldst intice
        Hell torments unto thee,
        And thine owne devill be.

9. O, what a dirty dunghill art thou growne,   50
    A nasty stinking kennell foule!

When thou awak'st and seest what thou hast done,
Sorrow will swallow up thy soule,
To think how thou art foyl'd,
And all thy glory spoyl'd.

10. Or if thou canst not be asham'd, at least   55
Have some compassion on thy self,
Before thou art transformèd all to beast ;[19]
At last strike saile, avoid the shelf[20]
Which in that gulfe doth lie,
Where all that enter die.   60

7. THE COVETOUSNESSE OF THE HEART.

Where your treasure is, there will your heart be also. Matt. vi. 21.

EPIGR. VII.

Dost thou enquire, thou heartlesse wanderer,
Where thine heart is ?   Behold, thine heart is here.
Here thine heart is where that is which above
Thine own deare heart thou dost esteem and love.

ODE VII.

1.   See the deceitfulnesse of sinne,
And how the devill cheateth worldly men ;
They heap up riches to themselves, and then
They think they cannot choose but winne,
Though for their parts   5
They stake their hearts.

2.   The merchant sends his heart to sea,
    And there together with his ship 'tis tost :
    If this by chance miscarry, that is lost,
       His confidence is cast away ;   10
          He hangs the head,
          As he were dead.

3.   The pedlar cryes, 'What doe you lack?
    What will you buy?' and boasts his wares the best :
    But offers you the refuse of the rest,   15
       As though his heart lay in his pack ;
          Which greater gaine
          Alone can draine.

4.   The plowman furrowes up his land,
    And sowes his heart together with his seed ;   20
    Which, both alike earth-borne, on earth doe feed,
       And prosper or are at a stand ;   └=born
          He and his field
          Like fruit doe yeeld.

5.   The broker and the scrivner have   25
    The us'rer's heart in keeping with his bands : =bonds
    His soul's deare sustenance lyes in their hands,
       And if they break, their shop's his grave :
          His int'rest is
          His only blisse.   30

6.   The money-horder in his bags
    Binds up his heart, and locks it in his chest ;

The same key serves to that and to his brest,
  Which of no other heaven brags,
      Nor can concert   35
      A joy so great.

7.   So for the greedy landmunger :[21]
  The purchases he makes in ev'ry part
 Take livery and seisin[22] of his heart;
      Yet his insatiate hunger,   40
        For all his store,
        Gapes after more.

8.   Poore wretched muckwormes, wipe your eyes;
  Uncase those trifles that besot you so;
  Your rich-appearing wealth is reall woe;   45
      Your death in your desires lyes;
        Your hearts are where
        You love and feare.

9.   Oh, think not then the world deserves
  Either to be belov'd or fear'd by you :   50
  Give heaven these affections as its due,
      Which alwayes what it hath preserves
        In perfect blisse,
        That endlesse is.

8. THE HARDNESSE OF THE HEART.

They made their hearts as an adamant stone, lest they should heare the
the Lord. Zech. vii. 12.

EPIGR. VIII.

Words move thee not, nor works, nor gifts, nor strokes;
Thy sturdy adamantine heart provokes
My justice, sleights My mercies : anvile-like,   =slights
Thou standst unmovèd, though My hammer strike.

ODE VIII.

1. What have we here ?   An heart ?   It lookes like one;
   The shape and colour speake it such :
   But having brought it to the touch,[23]
   I find it is no better then a stone :
         Adamants are   5
         Softer by farre.

2. Long hath it steepèd been in mercie's milke,
   And soakèd in salvation ;
   Meet for the alteration
   Of anvills, to have made them soft as silke ;   10
         Yet it is still
         Hard'ned in ill.

3. Oft have I rain'd My word upon it, oft
   The dew of heaven hath distill'd,
   With promises of mercy fill'd,   15
   Able to make mountaines of marble soft ;
         Yet it is not
         Changèd a jot.

4. My beames of love shine on it every day,
    Able to thaw the thickest ice,   20
    And where they enter, in a trice
To make congealèd crystall melt away ;
            Yet warme they not
            This frozen clot.

5. Nay more ; this hammer, that is wont to grind   25
    Rocks into dust and powder small,
    Makes no impression at all,
Nor dint, nor crack, nor flaw that I can find ;
            But leaves it as
            Before it was.   30

6. Is Mine Almighty arme decai'd in strength ?
    Or hath Mine hammer lost its weight,
    That a poore lumpe of earth should sleight
My mercies, and not feele My wrath at length,
            With which I make   slight, l. 33   35
            Ev'n heav'n to shake ?

7. No ; I am still the same, I alter not,
    And when I please, My workes of wonder
    Shall bring the stoutest spirits under,
And make them to confesse it is their lot   40
            To bow or break
            When I but speak.

8. But I would have men know 'tis not My Word
    Or works alone can change their hearts;
    These instruments performe their parts,   45
But 'tis My Spirit doth this fruit afford.
      'Tis I, not art,
      Can melt man's heart.

9. Yet would they leave their customary sinning,
    And so unclench the devill's clawes,   50
    That keepes them captive in his pawes,
My bounty soone should second their beginning;
      Ev'n hearts of steel
      My force should feel.

9. THE DIVISION OF THE HEART.

Their heart is divided; now shall they be found faulty. Hosea x. 2.

EPIGR. IX.

Vaine trifling virgin! I Myselfe have given
Wholly to thee; and shall I now be driven
To rest contented with a petty part,
That have deservèd more then a whole heart?

ODE IX.

1. More mischiefe yet! Was't not enough before
    To robbe Me wholly of thine heart,
      Which I alone
      Should call Mine owne,
    But thou must mock Me with a part?   5
Crowne injury with scorne to make it more?

2. What's a whole heart?   Scarce flesh enough to serve
    A kite one breakfast.   How much lesse,
        If it should be
        Offer'd to Me,   10
    Could it sufficiently expresse
What I for making it at first deserve !

3. I gave 't thee whole, and fully furnishèd
    With all its faculties entire ;
        There wanted not   15
        The smallest jot
    That strictest justice could require
To render it compleatly perfected.

4. And is it reason, what I gave in grosse[24]
    Should be return'd but by retaile ?   20
        To take so small
        A part for all,
    I reckon of no more availe
Then where I scatter gold to gather drosse.

5. Give Me thine heart but[25] as I gave it thee :   25
    Or give it Me at least as I
        Have given Mine
        To purchase thine:
    I halv'd it not when I did die,
But gave Myself wholly to set thee free.   30

6. The heart I gave thee was a living heart;
　　And when thine heart by sinne was slaine,
　　　　I laid downe Mine
　　　　To ransome thine;
　　That thy dead heart might live againe,　　35
　And live entirely perfect, not in part.

7. But whilst thine heart's divided it is dead—
　　Dead unto Me, unlesse it live
　　　　To Me alone;
　　　　It is all one　　　　　　40
　　To keepe all and a part to give;
　For what's a body worth without an head?

8. Yet this is worse, that what thou keepst from Me
　　Thou dost bestow upon My foes;
　　　　And those not Mine　　　45
　　　　Alone, but thine—
　　The proper causes of thy woes,
　For whom I gave My life to set thee free.

9. Have I betroth'd thee to Myself, and shall
　　The devill and the world intrude　　50
　　　　Upon My right
　　　　Ev'n in My sight?
　　Think not thou canst Me so delude;
　I will have none unlesse I may have all.

10. I made it all, I gave it all to thee,   55
    I gave all that I had for it ;
        If I must loose,
        I'll rather choose
    Mine interest in all to quit :
Or keep it whole, or give it whole to Me.   60

10. THE INSATIABLENESSE OF THE HEART.

Who inlargeth his desire as hell, and is as death, and cannot be satisfied.
Habakuk ii. 5.

EPIGR. X.

The whole round world is not enough to fill
The heart's three corners ; but it craveth still.
Onely the Trinity, that made it, can
Suffice the vast-triangled heart of man.

ODE X.

1. The thirsty earth and barren wombe cry, Give ;
    The grave devoureth all that live ;
    The fire still burneth on, and never saith,
      It is enough ; the horseleech hath
Many more daughters.   But the heart of man   5
Outgapes them all, as much as heav'n one span.

2. Water hath drown'd the earth ; the barren wombe
    Hath teem'd sometimes, and been the tombe
    To its owne swelling issue ; and the grave
      Shall one day a sicke surfeit have ;   10

When all the fuell is consum'd, the fire
Will quench itselfe, and of itself expire.

3. But the vast heart of man's insatiate :
    His boundlesse appetites dilate
Themselves beyond all limits ; his desires   15
    Are endlesse still, whilst he aspires
To happinesse, and faine would find that treasure
Where it is not—his wishes know no measure.

4. His eye with seeing is not satisfièd,
    Nor 's eare with hearing : he hath trièd   20
At once to furnish ev'ry sev'rall sense
    With choise of curious objects, whence
He might extract, and into one unite
A perfect quintessence of all delight.

5. Yet having all that he can fancy, still   25
    There wanteth something more to fill
His empty appetite.   His mind is vext,
    And he is inwardly perplext.
He knowes not why ; whereas the truth is this,
He would find something there where nothing is.

6. He rambles over all the faculties ;   31
    Ransacks the secret treasuries
Of art and nature ; spells the universe
    Letter by letter ; can reherse
All the records of time ; pretends to know   35
Reasons of all things, why they must be so.

7. Yet is not so contented, but would faine
    Prie in God's cabinet,[26] and gaine
Intelligence from heav'n of things to come;
    Anticipate the day of doome;   40
And read the issues of all actions so,
As if God's secret counsells he did know.

8. Let him have all the wealth, all the renowne
    And glory that the world can crowne
Her dearest darlings with; yet his desire   45
    Will not rest there, but still aspire:
Earth cannot hold him, nor the whole creation
Containe his wishes or his expectation.

9. The heart of man's but little, yet this All[27]
    Comparèd thereunto 's but small;   50
Of such a large unparallel'd extense
    Is the short-lin'd circumference[28]
Of that three-corner'd figure, which to fill
With the round world is to leave empty still.

10. Go, greedy soule, addresse thyselfe to heav'n, 55
    And leave the world as 'tis, bereav'n
Of all true happinesse, or any thing
    That to thine heart content can bring;
But there a trine-une God in glory sits,
Who all grace-trusting hearts both fills and fits. 60

11. THE RETURNING OF THE HEART.

Remember this, and shew yourselves men: bring it again to heart, O ye transgressors. Isay. xlvi. 8.

EPIGR. XI.

Oft have I call'd thee : O returne at last,
Returne unto thine heart ; let the time past
Suffice thy wanderings ; know, that to cherish
Revolting still is a meer will to perish.

ODE XI.

1. *Christ.*

Returne, O wanderer, returne, returne ;
    Let Me not alwayes wast My words in vaine,
As I have done too long.   Why dost thou spurn
    And kick the counsells that should bring thee back
        again ?

2. *The Soule.*

What's this that checks my course ? Methinks I feel 5
    A cold remissnesse seising on my mind ;
My stagger'd resolutions seem to reel,
    As though they had in hast forgot mine heart behind.

3. *Christ.*

Returne, O wanderer, returne, returne,
    Thou art already gone too farre away :   10
It is enough ; unlesse thou meane to burne
    In hell for ever, stop thy course at last, and stay.

4. *The Soule.*

There's something holds me back ; I cannot move
    Forward one foot ; methinks the more I strive
The lesse I stirre.   Is there a pow'r above   15
    My will in me, that can my purposes reprive ?[29]

5. *Christ.*

No power of thine own ; 'tis I that lay
    Mine hand upon thine haste ; Whose will can make
The restlesse motions of the heavens stay,
    Stand still, turne back againe, or new-found courses
        take.   .   20

6. *The Soule.*

What ! am I riveted or rooted here,
    That neither forward nor on either side
I can get loose?   Then there's no hope, I feare,
    But I must back againe, whatever me betide.

7. *Christ.*

And back again thou shalt ; I'll have it so.   25
    Though thou hast hitherto My voyce neglected,
Now I have handed thee, I'll have thee know,
    That what I will have done shall not be uneffected.

8-14. *The Soule.*

Thou wilt prevaile, then, and I must returne ;
    But how? or whither? when a world of shame 30
And sorrow lies before me, and I burne
    With horror in myself to think upon the same.

Shall I returne to Thee? Alas, I have
　　No hope to be receiv'd; a runne-away,
A rebell to returne! mad-men may rave 　　　　35
　　Of mercy-miracles, but what will Justice say?

Shall I returne to mine owne heart? Alas,
　　'Tis lost and dead and rotten long ago;
I cannot find it what at first it was,
　　And it hath been too long the cause of all my woe. 40

Shall I forsake my pleasures and delights,
　　My profits, honours, comforts, and contents,
For that the thought whereof my mind affrights,
　　Repentant sorrow, that the soule asunder rents?

Shall I returne, that cannot though I would? 　　　45
　　I, that had strength enough to go astray,
Find myself faint and feeble now I should
　　Returne; I cannot runne, I cannot creep this way.

What shall I doe? Forward I must not goe,
　　Backward I cannot; if I tarry here 　　　　50
I shall be drownèd in a world of woe,
　　And antidate mine own damnation by despaire.[30]

But is 't not better hold that which I have,
　　Then unto future expectation trust?
O no, to reason thus is but to rave; 　　　　55
　　Therefore returne I will, because returne I must.

15. *Christ.*

Returne, and welcome; if thou wilt thou shalt :
Although thou canst not of thyselfe, yet I
That call, can make thee able. Let the fault
Be Mine, if when thou wilt returne I let thee lie. 6o

12. THE POWRING OUT OF THE HEART.

Powre out thine heart like water before the face of the Lord. Lam. ii. 19.

Epigr. XII.

Why dost thou hide thy wounds? why dost thou hide
In thy close breast thy wishes, and so side
With thine owne soares and sorrowes?   Like a spout
Of water let thine heart to God break out.

Ode XII.

1. *The Soule.*

Can death or hell be worse then this estate?
Anguish, amazement, horror, and confusion
Drowne my distracted mind in deep distresses.³¹
My grief's grown so transcendent, that I hate
To heare of comfort, as a false conclusion   5
Vainly inferr'd from feignèd premises.
    What shall I do? what strange course shall I try,
    That, though I loath to live, yet dare not die?
                         [=I that (l. 8)

2. *Christ.*

Be rul'd by Me; I'll teach thee such a way
As that thou shalt not onely draine thy mind   10

From that destructive deluge of distresse
That overwhelmes thy thoughts, but clear the day,
And soone recover light, and strength to find
And to regaine thy long-lost happiness.

 Confesse, and pray. Say what it is doth aile thee, 15
 What thou wouldst have, and that shall soon avail
  thee.[32]

3-7. *The Soule.*

' Confesse, and pray'?   If that be all, I will.
Lord, I am sick, and Thou art health; restore me.
Lord, I am weake, and Thou art strength; sustaine me.
Thou art all goodnesse, Lord; and I all ill.   20
Thou, Lord, art holy; I uncleane before Thee.
Lord, I am poor, and Thou art rich; maintaine me.
 Lord, I am dead, and Thou art life; revive me.
 Justice condemnes; let mercy, Lord, reprieve[33] me.

A wretched miscreant I am, compos'd   25
Of sinne and misery; 'tis hard to say
Which of the two allyes me most to hell :
Native corruption makes me indispos'd
To all that's good, but apt to go astray ;
Prone to doe ill, unable to doe well.   30
 My light is darkenesse, and my liberty
 Bondage; my beauty foule deformity.

A plague of leprosic o'rspreadeth all
My pow'rs and faculties; I am uncleane,
I am uncleane : my liver broyles with lust; 35
Rancor and malice overflow my gall ;

Envy my bones doth rot and keep me leane ;
Revengefull wrath makes me forget what's just :
    Mine care's uncircumcis'd, mine eye is evill ;
    And hating goodnesse makes me parcell-devill.[34]   40

My callous conscience is cauteriz'd ;
My trembling heart shakes with continuall feare ;
My frantick passions fill my mind with madnesse ;
My windy thoughts with pride are tympaniz'd ; =swollen
My poys'nous tongue spits venome ev'ry where ;   45
My wounded spirit's swallow'd up with sadnesse ;
    Impatient discontentment plagues me so,
    I neither can stand still nor forward goe.

Lord, I am all diseases : hospitalls
And bills of mountebanks have not so many,   50
Nor halfe so bad. Lord, heare, and help, and heale me.
Although my guiltinesse for vengeance calls,
And colour of excuse I have not any ;
Yet Thou hast goodnesse, Lord, that may availe me.
    Lord, I have powr'd out all my heart to Thee : 55
    Vouchsafe one drop of mercy unto me.

13. THE CIRCUMCISION OF THE HEART.

Circumcise the foreskin of your heart, and be no more stiffnecked.
Devt. x. 16.

Epigr. XIII.

Here, take thy Saviour's crosse, the nailes, and speare,
That for thy sake His holy flesh did teare ;

Use them as knives thine heart to circumcise,
And dresse[35] thy God a pleasing sacrifice.

Ode XIII.

1. Heale thee? I will. But first I'll let thee know
        What it comes to.
The plaister was preparèd long agoe :
        But thou must doe
        Something thyselfe, that it may bee   5
        Effectually apply'd to thee.

2. I, to that end, that I might cure thy sores,
        Was slaine, and dy'd ;
By Mine owne people was turn'd out of doores,
        And crucify'd ;   10
        My side was piercèd with a speare,
        And nailes My hands and feet did teare.

3. Doe thou then to thyselfe as they to Mee :
        Make haste, and try
The old man that is yet alive in thee   15
        To crucifie ;
        Till he be dead in thee My blood
        Is like to doe thee little good.

4. My course of physick is to cure the soule
        By killing sinne.   20
So then thine own corruptions to controule
        Thou must beginne ;

Untill thine heart be circumcis'd,
My death will not be duly priz'd.

5. Consider then My crosse, My nailes and speare,   25
    And let that thought
Cut rasor-like thine heart, when thou dost heare
    How deare I bought
    Thy freedome from the pow'r of sinne,
    And that distresse which thou wast in.   30

6. Cut out the iron sinew of thy neck,
    That it may be
Supple and pliant to obey My beck ;[36]
    And learne of Me.
    Meeknesse alone, and yeelding, hath   35
    A power to appease My wrath.

7. Shave off thine hairy scalpe, those curlèd locks
    Powd'red with pride ;
Wherewith thy scornfull heart My judgements mocks,
    And thinks to hide   40
    Its thunder-threatned head, which bared[37]
    Alone is likely to be spared.

8. Rippe off those seeming robes, but reall rags,
    Which earth admires
As honourable ornaments, and brags[38]   45
    That it attires,—
    Cumbers thee with indeed. Thy sores
    Fester with what the world adores.

9. Clip thine Ambition's wings, let downe thy plumes ;
    And learne to stoope   50
Whilst thou hast time to stand. Who still presumes
    Of strength will droope
    At last, and flagge when he should flye :
    Falls hurt them most that climbe most high.

10. Scrape off that scaly scurffe of vanities   55
    That clogges thee so ;
Profits and pleasures are those enemies
    That worke thy woe :
    If thou wilt have Me cure thy wounds,
    First ridde each humor that abounds.   60

14. THE CONTRITION OF THE HEART.

A broken and contrite heart, O God, Thou wilt not despise. Psalm li. 17.

Epigr. XIV.

How gladly would I bruise and breake this heart
Into a thousand pieces, till the smart
Make it confesse that of its owne accord
It wilfully rebell'd against the Lord !

Ode XIV.

1. Lord, if I had an arme of pow'r like Thine,
    And could effect what I desire,
    My love-drawne heart, like smallest wyre
Bended and writhen,[39] should together twine,

I.

And twisted stand   5
With Thy command.
Thou shouldst no sooner bid, but I would goe ;
Thou shouldst not will the thing I would not doe.

2. But I am weake, Lord, and corruption strong :
    When I would faine doe what I should,   10
    Then I cannot doe what I would—
Mine action's short, when mine intention's long ;
        Though my desire
        Be quick as fire,
Yet my performance is as dull as earth,   15
And stifles its own issue in the birth.

3. But what I can doe, Lord, I will, since what
    I would I cannot ; I will try
    Whether mine heart, that's hard and dry,
Being calm'd and temperèd⁴⁰ with that   20
        Liquor which falls
        From mine eye-balls,
Will worke more pliantly, and yeeld to take
Such new impression as Thy grace shall make.

4. In mine owne conscience then, as in a mortar,   25
    I'll place mine heart, and bray it there ;
    If griefe for what is past and feare
Of what's to come be a sufficient torture,
        I'll breake it all
        In pieces small ;   30

Sinne shall not finde a sheard[41] without a flaw
Wherein to lodge one lust against Thy law.

5. Remember then, mine heart, what thou hast done,
　　What thou hast left undone; the ill
　　Of all my thoughts, words, deeds, is still　35
Thy cursèd issue onely; thou art growne
　　　　To such a passe,
　　　　That never was,
Nor is, nor will there be a sinne so bad,
But thou some way therein an hand hast had.　40

6. Thou hast not been content alone to sinne,
　　But hast made others sinne with thee;
　　Yea, made their sinnes thine owne to be,
By liking and allowing them therein :
　　　　Who first beginnes,　　　　45
　　　　Or followes, sinnes—
Not his owne sinnes alone, but sinneth o're
All the same sinnes, both after and before.

7. What boundlesse sorrow can suffice a guilt
　　Growne so transcendent ?　Should thine eye 50
　　Weepe seas of blood, thy sighes outvie
The winds when with the waves they run at tilt,
　　　　Yet they could not
　　　　Cancel one blot ;
The least of all thy sinnes against thy God　55
Deserves a thunderbolt should be thy rod.

8. Break then, mine heart; and since thou cannot grieve
    Enough at once while thou art whole,
    Shiver thyself to dust, and dole[42]
Thy sorrow to thy sev'rall atomes; give   60
    All to each part,
    And by that art
Strive thy dissever'd self to multiply,
And want of weight with number to supply.

15. THE HUMILIATION OF THE HEART.

The patient in spirit is better then the proud in spirit.   Eccl. vii. 9.

EPIGR. XV.

Mine heart, alas, exalts itself too high,
And doth delight a loftier pitch to flye
Then it is able to maintaine, unlesse
It feel the weight of Thine imposèd presse.

ODE XV.

1. So let it be,
        Lord, I am well content;
    And Thou shalt see
        The time is not mis-spent   [quell
    Which Thou dost then bestow, when Thou dost
    And crush the heart that pride before did swell. 6

2. Lord, I perceive
        As soone as Thou dost send,
    And I receive
        The blessings Thou dost lend,   10

Mine heart begins to mount,[43] and doth forget
The ground whereon it goes, where it is set.

3. In health I grew
    Wanton ; began to kick,
  As though I knew   15
    I never should be sick :
  Diseases take me downe, and make me know
  Bodies of brasse must pay the death they owe.

4. If I but dreame
    Of wealth, mine heart doth rise   20
  With a full streame
    Of pride ; and I despise
  All that is good, untill I wake and spie
  The swelling bubble prickt with poverty.

5. A little wind   25
    Of undeservèd praise
  Blowes up my mind ;[44]
    And my swoll'n thoughts doth raise
  Above themselves, untill the sense of shame
  Makes me contemne my self-dishonour'd name. 30

6. One moment's mirth
    Would make me run starke mad ;
  And the whole earth,
    Could it at once be had,
  Would not suffice my greedy appetite,   35
  Didst Thou not paine instead of pleasure write.

7. Lord, it is well
   I was in time brought downe,
   Else Thou canst tell
      Mine heart would soone have flown   40
   Full in Thy face, and studi'd to requite
   The riches of Thy goodnesse with despight.

8. Slack not Thine hand :
   Lord, turne Thy screw about ;
   If Thy presse stand,   45
      Mine heart may chance slip out.
   O quest[45] it unto nothing, rather then
   It should forget itselfe, and swell again.

9. Or if Thou art
   Dispos'd to let it goe ;   50
   Lord, teach mine heart
      To lay itselfe as low
   As Thou canst cast it, that prosperity
   May still be temper'd with humility.

10. Thy way to rise   55
      Was to descend : let me
   Myselfe despise,
      And so ascend with Thee.   [high,
   Thou throwst them down that lift themselves on
   And raisest them that on the ground doe lie.   60

16. THE SOFTENING OF THE HEART.

God maketh my heart soft. Iob xxiii. 16.

EPIGR. XVI.

Mine heart is of itself a marble ice,
Both cold and hard.   But Thou canst in a trice
Melt it like waxe, great God, if from above
Thou kindle in it once Thy fire of love.

ODE XVI.

1.   Nay, blessed Founder, leave me not,
          If out of all this grot
      There can but any gold be got.
      The time Thou dost bestow, the cost
              And paines will not be lost :   5
      The bargaine is but hard at most ;
And such are all those Thou dost make with me,
Thou knowst Thou canst not but a loser be.

2.   When the sun shines with glitt'ring beames,
              His cold-dispelling gleames   10
      Turne snow and ice to wat'ry streames ;
      The waxe, as soone as it hath smelt
          The warmth of fire, and felt
      The glowing heat thereof, will melt ;
Yea, pearles with vinegar dissolve we may,[46]   15
And adamants[47] in bloud of goats, they say.

3.   If Nature can doe this, much more,
              Lord, may Thy grace restore
      Mine heart to what it was before :

There's the same matter in it still,   20
          Though new-inform'd with ill,
     Yet can it not resist Thy will;
Thy pow'r, that fram'd it at the first, as oft
As Thou wilt have it, Lord, can make it soft.

4.   Thou art the Sun of Righteousnesse !   25
          And though I must confesse
     Mine heart's growne hard in wickednesse,
          Yet Thy resplendent rayes of light,
               When once they come in sight,
          Will quickly thawe what froze by night :   30
Lord, in Thine healing wings a pow'r doth dwell
Able to melt the hardest heart in hell.

5.   Although mine heart in hardnesse passe
          Both iron, steel, and brasse,
     Yea, th' hardest thing that ever was,   35
          Yet if Thy fire Thy Spirit accord,
               And working with Thy Word
          A blessing unto it afford,
It will grow liquid, and not drop alone,
But melt itself away before Thy throne.   40

6.   Yea, though my flinty heart be such
          That the sun cannot touch,
     Nor fire sometimes affect it much,
          Yet Thy warme-reeking self-shed bloud,
               O Lamb of God, 's so good   45
          It cannot alwayes be withstood.

That aqua-regia[48] of Thy love prevailes,
Ev'n where Thy power's aqua-fortis[49] failes.

7.   Then leave me not so soon, dear Lord,
            Though I neglect Thy Word,   50
       And what Thy power doth afford;
       Yet try Thy mercy and Thy love,
            The force thereof may move
       When all things else successlesse prove :
Soakt in Thy bloud, mine heart will soone surrender
Its native hardness, and grow soft and tender.   56

17. THE CLEANSING OF THE HEART.

O Jerusalem, wash thine heart from wickednesse, that thou maist be
saved. Ier. v. 14.

EPIGR. XVII.

Ovt of thy wounded husband's Saviour's side,
Espousèd soul, there flowes with a full tide
A fountaine for uncleannesse : wash thee there,
Wash there thine heart, and then thou needst not feare.

ODE XVII.

1.   O endlesse misery !
       I labour still, but still in vaine :
            The staines of sinne I see
       Are vaded[50] all, or di'd in graine ;
            There's not a blot   5
            Will stirre a jot

For all that I can doe ;
There is no hope
In fuller's sope,
Though I adde nitre too.   10

2.   I many wayes have tri'd,
Have often soakt it in cold feares,
And, when a time I spi'd,
Powrèd upon it scalding teares ;
Have rins'd and rub'd,   15
And scrapt and scrub'd,
And turn'd it up and downe :
Yet can I not
Wash out one spot ;
It's rather fouler growne.   20

3.   O miserable state !
Who would be troubled with an heart
As I have been of late,
Both to my sorrow, shame, and smart ?
If it will not   25
Be cleaner got,
'Twere better I had none ;
Yet how should we
Divided be,
That are not two, but one !   30

4.   But am I not starke-wilde,[51]
That go about to wash mine heart

With hands that are defil'd
As much as any other part?
    Whilst all thy teares,   35
    Thine hopes and feares,
    Both ev'ry word and deed
    And thought is foule,
    Poore silly soule,
    How canst thou looke to speed?   40

5.   Can there no helpe be had?
Lord, Thou art holy, Thou art pure:
    Mine heart is not so bad,
So foule, but Thou canst cleanse it sure.
    Speak, blessed Lord,   45
    Wilt Thou afford
    Me meanes to make it cleane?
    I know Thou wilt;
    Thy blovd were spilt
    Should it runne still in vaine.   50

6.   Then to that blessed spring,
Which from my Saviour's sacred side
    Doth flow, mine heart I'll bring;
And there it will be purifi'd:
    Although the dye   55
    Wherein I lie,
    Crimson or scarlet were,
    This bloud, I know,

Will make 't, as snow
Or wooll, both cleane and cleere.   60

18. THE GIVING OF THE HEART.

My sonne, give Me thine heart. Prov. xxiii. 21.

EPIGR. XVIII.

The onely love, the onely feare, Thou art,
Dear and dread Saviour, of my sin-sick heart :
Thine heart Thou gavest that it might be mine ;
Take Thou mine heart, then, that it may be Thine.

ODE XVIII.

1. Give Thee mine heart?   Lord, so I would,
    And there's great reason that I should,
       If it were worth the having ;
    Yet sure Thou wilt esteem that good
    Which Thou hast purchas'd with Thy bloud,   5
       And thought it worth the craving.

2. Give Thee mine heart?   Lord, so I will,
    If Thou wilt first impart the skill
       Of bringing it to Thee ;
    But should I trust myself to give   10
    Mine heart, as sure as I doe live
       I should deceivèd be.

3. As all the value of mine heart
    Proceeds from favour, not desert,
       Acceptance is its worth ;   15

So neither know I how to bring
A present to my heav'nly King,
   Unlesse He set it forth.

4. Lord of my life, methinkes I heare
   Thee say that Thee alone to feare,   20
      And Thee alone to love,
   Is to bestow mine heart on Thee;
   That other giving none can be
      Whereof Thou wilt approve.

5. And well Thou dost deserve to be   25
   Both lovèd, Lord, and fear'd by me,
      So good, so great Thou art;
   Greatnesse so good, goodnesse so great,
   As passeth all finite conceit,
      And ravisheth mine heart.   30

6. Should I not love Thee, blessed Lord,
   Who freely of Thine own accord
      Laidst downe Thy life for me?
   For me, that was not dead alone,
   But desp'ratly transcendent grown   35
      In enmitie to Thee.

7. Should I not feare before Thee, Lord,
   Whose hand spannes heaven; at Whose word
      Devills themselves doe quake?
   Whose eyes out-shine the sunne, Whose beck 40
   Can the whole course of nature check,
      And its foundations shake?

8. Should I with-hold mine heart from Thee,
  The fountaine of felicity;
      Before Whose presence is　　　　　45
  Fulnesse of joy; at Whose right hand
  All pleasures in perfection stand,
      And everlasting blisse?

9. Lord, had I hearts a million,
  And myriads in ev'ry one　　　　　50
      Of choicest loves and feares,
  They were too little to bestow
  On Thee, to Whom all things I owe;
      I should be in arreares.

10. Yet since mine heart's the most I have,　55
  And that which Thou dost chiefely crave,
      Thou shalt not of it misse;
  Although I cannot give it so
  As I should doe, I'll offer't, though:
      Lord, take it, here it is.　　　　　60

19. THE SACRIFICE OF THE HEART.

The sacrifices of God are a broken heart. Psal. li. 17.

Epigr. XIX.

Nor calves nor bulls are sacrifices good
Enough for Thee, Who gav'st for me Thy bloud,
And more then that, Thy life: take Thine own part;
Great God, that gavest all, here, take mine heart.

Ode XIX.

1.   Thy former covenant of old,
Thy law of ordinances, did require
    Fat sacrifices from the fold,
And many other off'rings made by fire;
    Whilst Thy first Tabernacle stood,   5
    All things were consecrate with bloud.

2.   And can Thy better Covenant,
Thy law of grace and truth by Jesus Christ,
    Its proper sacrifices want
For such an Altar and for such a Priest?   10
    No, no; Thy Gospell doth require
    Choyse off'rings, too, and made by fire.

3.   A sacrifice for sinne indeed,
Lord, Thou didst make Thyself, and once for all;
    So that there never will be need   15
Of any more sin-off'rings, great or small;
    The life-bloud Thou didst shed for me
    Hath set my soule for ever free.

4.   Yea, the same sacrifice Thou dost
Still offer in behalfe of Thine elect;   20
    And to improve[52] it to the most,
Thy Word and Sacraments doe in effect
    Offer Thee oft, and sacrifice
    Thee daily in our eares and eyes.

5.   Yea, each beleeving soule may take   25
Thy sacrificèd flesh and bloud by faith
    And therewith an atonement make
For all its trespasses, Thy Gospell saith;
    Such infinite transcendent price
    Is there in Thy sweet sacrifice.   30

6.   But is this all?   Must there not be
Peace-offerings and sacrifices of
    Thanksgiving tenderèd unto Thee?
Yes, Lord, I know I should but mock and scoffe
    Thy sacrifice for sinne, should I   35
    My sacrifice of praise deny.

7.   But I have nothing of mine owne
Worthy to be presented in Thy sight;
    Yea, the whole world affords not one
Ox, ramme, or lambe wherein Thou canst delight:
    Lesse then myself it must not be;   41
    For thou didst give Thyself for me.

8.   Myself then I must sacrifice;
And so I will—mine heart, the onely thing
    Thou dost above all other prize   45
As Thine owne part, the best I have to bring:
    An humble heart's a sacrifice
    Which I know Thou wilt not despise.

9.   Lord, be my altar; sanctifie
Mine heart, Thy sacrifice; and let Thy Spirit 50

Kindle Thy fire of love, that I,
Burning with zeale to magnifie Thy merit,
May both consume my sinnes, and raise
Eternall trophies to Thy praise.

20. THE WEIGHING OF THE HEART.

The Lord pondereth the heart. Prov. xxi. 2.

EPIGR. XX.

The heart Thou giv'st as a great gift, my love,
Brought to the triall, nothing such will prove,
If Justice' equall ballance tell thy sight
That, weighèd with My Law, it is too light.

ODE XX.

1.   'Tis true, indeed, an heart
           Such as it ought to be,
      Entire and sound in ev'ry part,
      Is always welcome unto Me;
He that would please Me with an offering   5
Cannot a better have, although he were a king.

2.   And there is none so poore,
           But if he will he may
      Bring Me an heart, although no more;
      And on Mine altar may it lay.   10
The sacrifice which I like best is such
As rich men cannot boast, and poore men need not
      grutch.   =grudge

M

3.   Yet ev'ry heart is not
            A gift sufficient ;
      It must be purg'd from ev'ry spot,   15
      And all to pieces must be rent ;
Though thou hast sought to circumcise and bruise 't,
It must be weigh'd too, or else I shall refuse 't.

4.   My ballances are just,
            My Law's an equall weight ;   20
      The beame is strong, and thou maist trust
      My steady hand to hold it straight :
Were thine heart equall to the world in sight,
Yet it were nothing worth if it should prove too
      light.

5.   And so thou seest it doth ;   25
            My pond'rous Law doth presse
      This scale ; but that, as fill'd with froth, .
      Tilts up, and makes no shew of stresse :
Thine heart is empty sure, or else it would
In weight as well as bulke better proportion hold.

6.   Search it, and thou shalt find   31
            It wants integrity,
      And is not yet so thorow lin'd
      With single-ey'd sincerity
As it should be ; some more humility   35
There wants to make it weight, and some more
      constancy ;

7.   Whilst windy vanity
            Doth puffe it up with pride,
        And double-fac'd hypocrisie
           Doth many empty hollowes hide ;   40
It is but good in part, and that but little :
Wav'ring unstaidnesse makes its resolutions brittle.

8.   The heart that in My sight
           As currant coyne would passe
        Must not be the least graine too light,   45
           But as it stampèd was :
Keep then thine heart till it be better growne,
And when it is full weight I'll take it for Mine owne.

9.   But if thou art asham'd
           To find thine heart so light,   50
        And art afraid thou shalt be blam'd,
           I'll teach thee how to set it right :
Adde to My Law My Gospell, and there see
My merits thine : and then the scales will equall be.

21. THE TRYING OF THE HEART.

The fining pot for silver and the furnace for gold ; but the Lord trieth the
hearts. Prov. xvii. 3.

Epigr. XXI.

Thine heart, My deer, more precious is then gold,
Or the most precious things that can be told ;
Provided first that My pure fire have tri'd[53]
Out all the drosse, and passe it purifi'd.

Ode XXI.

1. 'What? Take it at adventure, and not try
 What metall it is made of?'   'No, not I.
     Should I now lightly let it passe,
 Take sullen[54] lead for silver, sounding brasse
         Instead of solid gold, alas,   5
 What would become of it?   In the great Day
 Of making jewells 'twould be cast away.'

2. The heart thou giv'st Me must be such a one
 As is the same throughout : I will have none
         But that which will abide the fire.   10
 'Tis not a glitt'ring outside I desire,
         Whose seeming shewes doe soone expire ;
 But reall worth within, which neither drosse
 Nor base allayes[55] make subject unto losse.

3. If in the composition of thine heart   15
 A stubborne steely wilfulnesse have part,
         That will not bow and bend to Me,
 Save onely in a meer formality
         Of tinsell-trim'd hypocrisie,
 I care not for it, though it shew as faire   20
 As the first blush of the sun-gilded aire.

4. The heart that in My furnace will not melt
 When it the glowing heat thereof hath felt,
         Turne liquid, and dissolve in teares
 Of true repentance for its faults—that heares   25
         My threatning voyce, and never feares—

Is not an heart worth having : if it be
An heart of stone, 'tis not an heart for Me.

5. The heart that, cast into My fornace, spits
   And sparkles in My face, falls into fits   30
      Of discontented grudging, whines
   When it is broken of its will, repines
      At the least suffering, declines
   My fatherly correction,—is an heart
   On which I care not to bestow Mine art.   35

6. The heart that in My flames asunder flies ;
   Scatters itselfe at random, and so lies
      In heapes of ashes here and there ;
   Whose dry dispersèd parts will not draw neer
      To one another, and adhere   40
   In a firme union, hath no metall in't
   Fit to be stamp'd and coynèd in My mint.

7. The heart that vapours out itselfe in smoak,
   And with those cloudy shadows thinkes to cloak
      Its empty nakednesse, how much   45
   So ever thou esteemest it, is such
      As never will endure My touch :[56]
   Before I tak't for Mine, then, I will trie
   What kind of metall in thine heart doth lie.

8. I'll bring it to My furnace, and there see   50
   What it will prove, what it is like to be.

If it be gold, it will be sure
The hottest fire that can be to endure,
　　And I shall draw it out more pure ;
Affliction may refine, but cannot wast,　　55
That heart wherein My love is fixèd fast.

22. THE SOUNDING OF THE HEART.

The heart is deceitfull above all things, and desperately wicked ; who can
know it ? I the Lord. Jer. xvii. 9.

Epigr. XXII.

I, that alone am infinite, can try
How deep within itselfe thine heart doth lie :
The sea-man's plummet can but reach the ground ;
I find that which thine heart itself ne'er found.

Ode XXII.

1. A goodly heart to see to, faire and fat?
　　　It may be so ; and what of that?
Is it not hollow ? Hath it not within
　　　A bottomlesse whirlpoole of sinne?
Are there not secret creeks and cranies there,　　5
　　　Turning and winding corners, where
The heart itself ev'n from itself may hide,
　　　And lurk in secret unespi'd?
I'll none of it, if such a one it prove ;
Truth in the inward parts is that I love.　　10

2. But who can tell what is within thine heart?
　　　'Tis not a worke of nature ; art

Cannot performe that taske ; 'tis I alone,
    Not man, to Whom man's heart is knowne.
Sound it thou maist, and must ; but then the line 15
    And plummet must be Mine, not thine ;
And I must guide it too ; thine hand and eye
    May quickly be deceiv'd ; but I,
That made thine heart at first, am better skill'd
To know when it is empty, when 'tis fill'd.   20

3. Lest then thou shouldst deceive thyself—for Me
    Thou canst not—I will let thee see
Some of those depths of Satan, depths of hell,
    Wherewith thine hollow heart doth swell :
Under pretence of knowledge in thy mind,   25
    Errour and ignorance I find ;
Quick-sands of rotten superstition,
    Spied over with misprision :[57]
Some things thou knowest not, misknowest others ;
And oft thy conscience its owne knowledge smothers.

4. Thy crooked will, that seemingly enclines   31
    To follow reason's dictates, twines
Another way in secret ; leaves its guide
    And laggs behind, or swarves aside ;   =swerves
Crab-like creeps backward ; when it should have made
    Progresse in good, is retrograde ;   36
Whilst it pretends a priviledge above
    Reason's prerogative, to move

As of itself unmov'd, rude passions learne
To leave the oare, and take in hand the sterne.[58]

5. The tides of thine affections ebbe and flow,   41
      Rise up aloft, fall downe below,
Like to the suddaine land-flouds, that advance
      Their swelling waters but by chance;
Thy love, desire, thy hope, delight, and feare,   45
      Ramble they care not when nor where;
Yet cunningly beare thee in hand,[59] they be
      Only directed unto Me,
Or most to Me, and would no notice take
Of other things, but only for My sake.   50

6. Such strange prodigious impostures lurke
      In thy prestigious[60] heart, 'tis worke
Enough for thee all thy life-time to learne
      How thou mayst truly it discerne;
That when upon Mine altar thou dost lay   55
      Thine off'ring, thou mayst safely say
And sweare it is an heart; for if it should
      Prove only an heart-case, it would
Nor pleasing be to Me, nor doe thee good;
An heart's no heart not rightly understood.   60

23. THE LEVELLING OF THE HEART.

Gladnesse to the upright in heart. Psal. xcvii. 11.

EPIGR. XXIII.

Set thine heart upright if thou wouldst rejoyce,
And please thyself in thine heart's pleasing choise;
But then be sure thy plumme and levell lie
Rightly appli'd to that which pleaseth Me.

ODE XXIII.

1. Nay, yet I have not done; one triall more
     Thine heart must undergo before
         I will accept of it,
             Unlesse I see
             It upright be,   5
         I cannot think it fit
     To be admitted in My sight,
And to partake of Mine eternall light. .

2. My will's the rule of righteousnesse, as free
     From errour as uncertainty;   10
         What I would have is just.
             Thou must desire
             What I require,
         And take it upon trust;
     If thou preferre thy will to Mine,   15
The levell's lost, and thou go'st out of line.

3. Dost thou not see how thine heart turnes aside,
     And leanes toward thyself? How wide

A distance there is here !
                Untill I see   20
                Both sides agree
            Alike with Mine, 'tis cleer
    The middle is not where 't should be ;
Likes something better, though it looke at Me.

4. I, that know best how to dispose of thee,   25
        Would have thy portion poverty,
            Lest wealth should make thee proud,
                And Me forget ;
                But thou hast set
            Thy voyce to cry aloud   30
        For riches, and unlesse I grant
    All that thou wishest thou complainst of want.

5. I, to preserve thine health, would have thee fast
        From Nature's daintics, lest at last
                Thy senses' sweet delight   35
                Should end in smart ;
                But thy vaine heart
            Will have its appetite
        Pleasèd to-day, though grief and sorrow
    Threaten to cancell all thy joyes to-morrow.   40

6. I, to prevent thine hurt by climing high,
        Would have thee be content to lie
                Quiet and safe below,
                Where peace doth dwell ;
                But thou dost swell   45

With vast desires, as though
A little blast of vulgar breath
Were better then deliverance from death.

7. I, to procure thine happinesse, would have
    Thee mercy at Mine hands to crave;   50
        But thou dost merit plead,
          And wilt have none
          But of thine owne,
        Till Justice strike thee dead:
    Thus still thy wand'ring wayes decline,   55
And all thy crooked paths go crosse to Mine.

24. THE RENEWING OF THE HEART.

A new heart will I give you, and a new spirit will I put within you.
Ezek. xxxvi. 26.

EPIGR. XXIV.

Art thou delighted with strange novelties,
Which often prove but old fresh-garnisht lies?
Leave then thine old, take the new heart I give thee,
Condemne thyself, that so I may reprieve thee.

ODE XXIV.

1.   No, no, I see
        There is no remedy;
    An heart that wants both weight and worth,
That's fill'd with naught but empty hollownesse,
And screw'd aside with stubborne wilfulnesse,   5
    Is onely fit to be cast forth;

Nor to be given Me,
　Nor kept by thee.

2.　　　　Then let it goe ;
　And if thou wilt bestow　　　　　　10
An acceptable heart on Me,
I'll furnish thee with one shall serve the turne
Both to be kept and given ; which will burne
　With zeale, yet not consumèd be,
　　Nor with a scornfull eye　　　　15
　　Blast standers by.

3.　　　　The heart that I
　Will give thee, though it lie
Buri'd in seas of sorrowes, yet
Will not be drown'd with doubt or discontent,　20
Though sad complaints sometimes may give a vent
　To grief, and teares the cheeks may wet ;
　　Yet it exceeds their art
　　To hurt this heart.

4.　　　　The heart I give,　　　　25
　Though it desire to live
And bath itself in all content,
Yet will not toyle or taint itself with any ;
Although it take a view and tast of many,
　It feeds on few, as though it meant　　30
　　To breakfast only here,
　　And dine elsewhere.

5.   This heart is fresh
   And new ; an heart of flesh,
  Not as thine old one was, of stone :   35
 A lively sp'ritly heart, and moving still,
 Active to what is good, but slow to ill ;
  An heart that with a sigh and grone
   Can blast all worldly joyes
    As trifling toyes.   40

6.   This heart is sound,
   And solid[61] will be found ;
  'Tis not an emptie ayrie flash
 That baites[62] at butterflies, and with full cry
 Opens at ev'ry flirting vanity :   45
  It sleights and scornes such paltry trash ; =slights
   But for eternity
    Dares live or die.

7.   I know thy mind ;
   Thou seekst content to find   50
  In such things as are new and strange.
 Wander no further, then ; lay by thine old,
 Take the new heart I give thee, and be bold
  To boast thyself of the exchange,
   And say that a new heart   55
    Exceeds all art.

25. THE ENLIGHTENING OF THE HEART.

They looked unto Him, and were lightened. Psalm xxxiv. 5.

Epigr. XXV.

Thou that art Light of lights, the onely sight
Of the blind world, lend me Thy saving light;
Disperse those mists, which in my soule have made
Darkenesse as deep as Hell's eternall shade.

Ode XXV.

1.   Alas, that I
  Could not before espie
 The soule-confounding misery
Of this more then Egyptian-dreadfull night!
 To be deprivèd of the light,   5
And to have eyes, but eyes devoid of sight,
 As mine have been, is such a woe
  As he alone can know
   That feeles it so.

2.   Darknesse hath been   10
  My God and me between
 Like an opacous[63] doubled skreen,
Through which nor light nor heat could passage find.
 Grosse ignorance hath made my mind
And understanding not bleer-ey'd, but blind; 15
 My will to all that's good is cold,
  Nor can I, though I would,
   Doe what I should.

3.   No, now I see
      There is no remedy   20
   Left in myself; it cannot be
That blind men in the darke should find the way
   To blessednesse, although they may
Imagine that high mid-night is noone-day,
     As I have done till now; they'll know   25
      At last, unto their woe,
        'Twas nothing so.

4.   Now I perceive
     Presumption doth bereave
   Men of all hope of helpe, and leave   30
Them, as it finds them, drown'd in misery,
   Despairing of themselves : to cry
For mercy is the only remedy
   That sinne-sicke soules can have; to pray
     Against this darknesse may   35
      Turne it to day.

5.   Then unto Thee,
     Great Lord of light, let me
   Direct my prayer that I may see.
Thou, that didst make mine eyes, canst soone restore
   That pow'r of sight they had before ;   41
And if Thou seest it good, canst give them more ;
   The night will quickly shine like day,
     If Thou doe but display
      One glorious ray.   45

6.   I must confesse,
        And I can doe no lesse,
    Thou art the Sun of Righteousnesse ;
There's healing in Thy wings ; Thy light is life,
    My darknesse death.   To end all strife   50
Be Thou mine husband ; let me be Thy wife ;
    Then both the light and life that's Thine,
        Though light and life divine,
            Will all be mine.

26. THE TABLE OF THE HEART.

I will put My law in their inward parts, and write it in their hearts.
Ier. xxxi. 33.

Epigr. XXVI.

In the soft table of thine heart I'll write
A new law, which I newly will indite.
Hard stony tables did containe the old,
But tender leaves of flesh shall this infold.

Ode XXVI.

1.   What will thy sight
        Availe thee, or My light,
    If there be nothing in thine heart to see
        Acceptable to Me ?
        A self-writ heart will not   5
    Please Me, or doe thee any good, I wot :
        The paper must be thine,
            The writing Mine.

2.   What I indite
'Tis I alone can write,   10
And write in books that I Myself have made.
'Tis not an easie trade
To read or write in hearts :
They that are skilfull in all other arts,
    When they take this in hand,   15
    Are at a stand.

3.   My Law of old
Tables of stone did hold,
Wherein I writ what I before had spoken ;
    Yet were they quickly broken :   20
    A signe the Covenant
Contain'd in them would due observance want ;
    Nor did they long remaine[64]
    Coppy'd again.   ·

4.   But now I'll try   25
What force in flesh doth lie ;
Whether thine heart renew'd afford a place
Fit for My law of grace.
This Covenant is better
Then that, though glorious, of the killing letter : 30
    This gives life—not by merit,
    But by My Spirit.

5.   When in men's hearts
And their most inward parts

N

I by My Spirit write My law of love,   35
  They then begin to move,
  Not by themselves, but Me ;
And their obedience is their liberty :
  There are no slaves but those
    That serve their foes.   40

6.   When I have writ
  My Covenant in it,
View thine heart by My light, and thou shalt see
  A present fit for Me.
The worth for which I look   45
Lies in the lines, not in the leaves, of th' book :
  Course paper may be lin'd   *coarse*
  With words refin'd.

7.   And such are Mine :
  No furnace can refine.   50
The choicest silver, so to make it pure,
  As My law put in ure,   *use*
  Purgeth the hearts of men ;
Which being rul'd and written with My pen—
  My Spirit—ev'ry letter   55
  Will make them better.

27. THE TILLING OF THE HEART.

I will turne unto you, and yee shall be tilled and sowne. Ezek. xxxvi. 9.

Epigr. XXVII.

Mine heart's a field; Thy crosse a plow; be pleas'd,
Dear Spouse, to till it, till the mould be rais'd
Fit for the seeding of Thy Word; then sow,
And if Thou shine upon it, it will grow.

Ode XXVII.

1.   So now methinks I find
  Some better vigour in my mind;
    My will begins to move,
  And mine affections stirre tow'rds things aboye;
  Mine heart growes bigge with hope; it is a field   5
    That some good fruit may yeeld,
  If it were till'd as it should be,
    Not by myself, but Thee.

2.   Great Husbandman, Whose pow'r
  All difficulties can devour,   10
    And doe what likes Thee best,
  Let not Thy field, mine heart, lie lay[65] and rest,   let
  Lest it be over-runne with noysome weeds,
    That spring of their own seeds:
  Unlesse Thy grace the growth should stoppe,   15
    Sinne would be all my croppe.

3.   Break up my fallow-ground,
  That there may not a clod be found

To hide one root of sinne :
Apply Thy plow be-time; now, now beginne   20
To furrow up my stiffe and starvy[66] heart ;
   No matter for the smart,
Although it roare when it is rent,
   Let not Thine hand relent.

4.   Corruptions rooted deep,   25
Showers of repentant teares must steep
   The mould to make it soft :
It must be stirr'd and turn'd, not once, but oft.
Let it have all its seasons ; O, impart
   The best of all Thine art ;   30
For of itself it is so tough,
   All will be but enough.

5.   Or, if it be Thy will
To teach me, let me learne the skill
   Myself to plow mine heart ;   35
The profit will be mine, and 'tis my part
To take the paines and labour, though th' encrease
   Without Thy blessing cease ;
If fit for nothing else, yet Thou
   Mayst make me draw Thy plow.   40

6.   Which of Thy plowes Thou wilt;
For Thou hast more then one.   My guilt,
   Thy wrath, Thy rods, are all
Plowes fit to teare mine heart to pieces small :

And when in these it apprehends Thee neer,   45
'Tis furrowèd with fear ;
Each weed turn'd under hides its head,
And showes as it were dead.

7.   But, Lord, Thy blessed Passion
Is a plow of another fashion,   50
Better then all the rest:
Oh, fasten me to that, and let the best
Of all my powers strive to draw it in,
And leave no roome for sinne ;
The vertue of Thy death can make   55
Sinne its fast hold forsake.

28. THE SEEDING OF THE HEART.

That on the good ground are they which, with an honest and good heart, having heard the Word, keep it, and bring forth fruit with patience. Lvke viii. 15.

EPIGR. XXVIII.

Lest the field of mine heart should unto Thee,
Great Husband-man that mad'st it, barren be,
Manure the ground, then come Thyself and seed it,
And let Thy servants water it and weed it.

ODE XXVIII.

1.   Nay, blessed Lord,
Unlesse Thou wilt afford
Manure as well as tillage to Thy field,
It will not yeeld

That fruit which Thou expectest it should beare : 5
    The ground I feare
    Will still remaine
Barren of what is good; and all the graine
    It will bring forth,
As of its owne accord, will not be worth   10
    The paines of gathering
    So poore a thing.

2.   Some faint desire,
        That quickly will expire,
Wither, and die, is all Thou canst expect ;   15
    If Thou neglect
To sow it now 'tis ready, Thou shalt find
    That it will blind
    And harder grow
Then at the first it was.   Thou must bestow   20
    Some further cost,
Else all Thy former labour will be lost ;
    Mine heart no corne will breed
    Without Thy seed.

3.   Thy word is seed,   25
        And manure[67] too ; will feed
As well as fill mine heart.   If once it were
    Well-rooted there,
It would come on apace ; O, then neglect
    No time, expect   30

No better season.
Now, now Thy field, mine heart, is ready ; reason
    Surrenders now ;
Now my rebellious will begins to bow,
      And mine affections are   35
        Tamer by farre.

        Lord, I have laine
      Barren too long, and faine
I would redeem the time, that I may be
    Fruitfull to Thee—   40
Fruitfull in knowledge, faith, obedience,
      Ere I goe hence ;
      That when I come
At harvest to be reapèd, and brought home,
      Thine angels may   45
My soule in Thy celestiall garner lay,
    Where perfect joy and blisse
      Eternall is.

      If to intreat
    A crop of purest wheat,   50
A blessing too transcendent should appeare
    For me to beare,
Lord, make me what Thou wilt, so Thou wilt take
    What Thou dost make,
      And not disdaine   55
To house me, though amongst Thy coursest graine ;

So I may be
Laid with the gleanings gatherèd by Thee,
When the full sheaves are spent,
I am content.   60

29. THE WATERING OF THE HEART.

I the Lord doe keep it.   I will water it every moment.   Isa. xxvii.].

EPIGR. XXIX.

Close downwards tow'rds the earth, open above
Tow'rds heaven, mine heart is.   O, let Thy love
Distill in fructifying dewes of grace,
And then mine heart will be a pleasant place.

ODE XXIX.

1.   See how this dry and thirsty land,
       Mine heart, doth gaping, gasping stand,
    And, close below, opens towards heav'n and Thee.
       Thou Fountaine of felicity,   [=closed
    Great Lord of living waters, water me ;   5
       Let not my breath that pants with paine
       Waste and consume itselfe in vaine.

2.   The mists that from the earth doe rise
       An heav'n-borne heart will not suffice ;   =born
    Coole it without they may, but cannot quench   10
       The scalding heat within, nor drench
    Its dusty dry desires, or fill one trench :
       Nothing but what comes from on high
       Can heav'n-bred longings satisfie.

See how the seed which Thou didst sow   15
Lies parch'd and wither'd, will not grow
Without some moisture; and mine heart hath none
    That it can truly call its owne,
By nature of itself more hard then stone;⁶ˢ
    Unlesse Thou water 't, it will lie   20
    Drownèd in dust, and still be dry.

Thy tender plants can never thrive
Whilst want of water doth deprive
Their roots of nourishment, which makes them call
    And cry to Thee, great All in All,   25
That seasonable show'rs of grace may fall,
    And water them : Thy Word will do 't,
    If Thou vouchsafe Thy blessing to 't.

O, then be pleasèd to unseal
Thy fountaine, blessed Saviour; deal   30
Some drops at least, wherewith my drooping spirits
    May be revivèd.   Lord, Thy merits
Yield more refreshing then the world inherits ;
    Rivers, yea seas, but ditches are,
    If with Thy springs one them compare.   35

If not whole show'rs of raine, yet, Lord,
A little pearly dew afford,
Begot by Thy celestiall influence
    On some chast vapour, raisèd hence
To be partaker of Thine excellence ;   40

A little, if it come from Thee,
Will be of great availe to me.

7.   Thou boundlesse Ocëan[69] of grace,
Let Thy free Spirit have a place
Within mine heart; full rivers then I know   45
Of living waters forth will flow,
And all Thy plants, Thy fruits and flow'rs will grow ;
Whilst Thy springs their roots doe nourish,
They must needs be fat, and flourish.

30. THE FLOWERS OF THE HEART.

My Beloved is gone downe into His garden, to the beds of spices, to feed in
the gardens and to gather lillies. Cant. vi. 2.

EPIGR. XXX.

Those lillies I doe consecrate to Thee,
Belovèd Spouse ; which spring, as Thou maist see,
Out of the seed Thou sowedst ; and the ground
Is better'd by Thy flow'rs when they abound.

ODE XXX.

1.   Is there a joy like this ?
What can augment my blisse ?
If my Belovèd will accept
A posie of these flowers, kept
And consecrated unto His content,   5
I hope hereafter He will not repent
The cost and paines He hath bestow'd
So freely upon me, that ow'd

Him all I had before,
And infinitly more.   10

Nay, try them, blessed Lord ;
Take them not on my word ;
But let the colour, tast, and smell
The truth of their perfections tell.
Thou that art infinite in wisdome, see   15
If they be not the same that came from Thee ;
If any difference be found,
It is occasion'd by the ground ;
Which yet I cannot see
So good as it should be.   20

What sayst Thou to that rose,
That queen of flowers, whose
Maidenly blushes fresh and faire
Out-brave the dainty morning aire ?
Dost Thou not in those lovely leaves espy   25
The perfect picture of that modesty,
That self-condemning shamefastnesse,
That is more ready to confesse
A fault, and to amend,
Then it is to offend ?   30

Is not this lilly pure ?
What fuller can procure
A white so perfect, spotlesse, clear,
As in this flower doth appear ?

Dost Thou not in this milky colour see   35
The lively lustre of sincerity ;
   Which no hypocrisie hath painted,
   Nor self-respecting ends have tainted ?
     Can there be to Thy sight
     A more entire delight?   40

5.   Or wilt Thou have beside
      Violets purple-di'd ?
   The sun-observing[70] marigold,
   Or orpin[71] never waxing old ;
The primrose, cowslip, gilliflow'r, or pinke,   45
Or any flow'r or herbe that I can think
   Thou hast a mind unto ? I shall
   Quickly be furnisht with them all,
     If once I doe but know
     That Thou wilt have it so.   50

6.   Faith is a fruitfull grace ;
      Well-planted, stores the place ;
   Fills all the borders, beds, and bow'rs
   With wholsome herbs and pleasant flow'rs.
Great Gard'ner, Thou saist, and I beleeve,   55
What Thou dost meane to gather Thou wilt give.
   Take then mine heart in hand to fill 't,
   And it shall yeeld Thee what Thou wilt ;
     Yea, Thou by gath'ring more
     Shalt still increase Thy store.   60

31. THE KEEPING OF THE HEART.

Keepe thy heart with all diligence. Prov. iv. 23.

EPIGR. XXXI.

Like to a garden that is closèd round,
That heart is safely kept which still is found
Compast with care, and guarded with the feare
Of God, as with a flaming sword and speare.

ODE XXXI.

1. *The Soule.*

Lord, wilt Thou suffer this?   Shall vermine spoile
  The fruit of all Thy toyle ;—
Thy trees, Thine herbs, Thy plants, Thy flowers thus ;
  And for an overplus
Of spite and malice overthrow Thy mounds,   5
  Lay common all Thy grounds?
Canst Thou endure Thy pleasant garden should
Be thus turn'd up as ordinary mould?

2. *Christ.*

What is the matter?   Why dost thou complaine?
  Must I as well maintaine   10
And keep as make thy fences?   Wilt thou take
  No paines for thine own sake?
Or doth thy self-confounding fancy feare thee,
  When there's no danger neer thee?
Speak out thy doubts and thy desires, and tell Me   15
What enemy or can or dares to quell thee?

3-6. *The Soule.*

Many and mighty and malicious, Lord,
  That seek with one accord
To work my speedy ruine ; and make haste
  To lay Thy garden waste :   20
The devill is a ramping[72] roaring lion,
  Hates at his heart Thy Zion ;
And never gives it respit day nor houre,
But still goes seeking whom he may devoure.

The world's a wildernesse, wherein I find   25
  Wild beasts of ev'ry kind—
Foxes and wolves and dogs and boares and beares;
  And which augments my feares,
Eagles and vultures and such birds of prey
  Will not be kept away ;   36
Besides the light-abhorring owles and bats,
And secret corner-creeping mice and rats.

But these, and many more, would not dismay
  Me much, unlesse there lay
One worse then all within ; myself I meane— 35
  My false, unjust, unclean,
Faithlesse, disloyall self, that both entice
  And entertaine each vice :
This homebred traiterous partaking's worse
Then all the violence of forain force.   40

Lord, Thou maist see my feares are grounded, rise
  Not from a bare surmise

Or doubt of danger only ; my desires
    Are but what need requires
Of Thy divine protection and defence   45
    To keep these vermine hence ;
Which, if they should not be restrain'd by Thee,
Would grow too strong to be kept out by me.

7. *Christ.*

Thy feare is just, and I approve thy care ;
    But yet thy comforts are   50
Provided for ev'n in that care and feare ;
    Whereby it doth appeare
Thou hast what thou desirest, My protection,
    To keep thee from defection :
The heart that cares and feares is kept by Me ;   55
I watch thee whilst thy foes are watch'd by thee.

32. THE WATCHING OF THE HEART.

I sleep, but my heart waketh. Cant. v. 2.

EPIGR. XXXII.

Whilst the soft bands of sleep tie up my sences,
My watchfull heart, free from all such pretences,
Searches for Thee, enquires of all about Thee ;
Nor day nor night able to be without Thee.

ODE XXXII.

1.   It must be so ; that God that gave
    Me senses and a mind would have

Me use them both, but in their severall kinds.
Sleep must refresh my senses, but my mind's
    A sparke of heav'nly fire, that feeds   5
    On action and employment, needs
No time of rest; for when it thinks to please
Itself with idlenesse, 'tis least at ease;
    Though quiet rest refresh the head,
    The heart that stirres not sure is dead.   10

2.   Whilst then my body ease doth take,
    My rest-refusing heart shall wake;
And that mine heart the better watch may keep,
I'll lay my senses for a time to sleep.
    Wanton desires shall not entice,   15
    Nor lust enveigle them to vice;
No fading colours shall allure my sight,
Nor sounds enchant mine eares with their delight;
    I'll bind my smell, my touch, my tast,
    To keep a strict religious fast.   20

3.   My worldly bus'nesse shall be still,
    That heav'nly thoughts my mind may fill;
My Marthae's cumb'ring cares shall cease their noise,
That Mary may attend her better choise;
    That meditation may advance   25
    Mine heart on purpose, not by chance,
My body shall keep holy day, that so
My mind with better liberty may goe

About her bus'nesse, and ingrosse
That gaine which worldly men count losse.   30

4.   And though my senses sleep the while,
      My mind my senses shall beguile
With dreams of Thee, dear Lord, Whose rare perfections
Of excellence are such that bare inspections
      Cannot suffice my greedy soule,   35
      Nor her fierce appetite controule ;
But that the more she lookes the more she longs,
And strives to thrust into the thickest throngs
      Of those divine discoveries,
      Which dazell even angels' eyes.   40

5.   Oh could I lay aside this flesh,
      And follow after Thee with fresh
And free desires, my disentangled soule,
Ravisht with admiration,[72] should roule
      Itself and all its thoughts on Thee ;   45
      And by beleeving strive to see,
What is invisible to flesh and blood,
And only by fruition understood,
      The beauty of each sev'rall grace
      That shines in Thy sunne-shaming face.   50

6.   But what I can doe that I will,
      Waking and sleeping, seek Thee still ;
I'll leave no place unpri'd into behind me
Where I can but imagine I may find Thee ;

I'le aske of all I meet, if they   55
Can tell me where Thou art : which way
Thou go'st, that I may follow after Thee ;   [me.
Which way Thou com'st, that Thou maist meet with
If not Thy face, Lord, let mine heart
Behold with Moses Thy back-part.·   6o

33. THE WOUNDING OF THE HEART.

He hath bent His bow, and set me as a mark for the arrow. Lam. iii. 12.

Epigr. XXXIII.

A thousand of Thy strongest shafts, my Light,
Draw up against this heart with all Thy might,
And strike it through : they that in need doe stand
Of cure are healèd by Thy wounding hand.

Ode XXXIII.

1. Nay, spare me not, dear Lord ; it cannot be
   They should be hurt that wounded are by Thee ;
       Thy shafts will heale the hearts they hit,
       And to each sore its salve will fit.
   All hearts by nature are both sick and sore,   5
   And mine as much as any else, or more ;
       There is no place that's free from sinne,
       Neither without it nor within ;
   And universall maladies doe crave
   Variety of medicines to have.   1o

2. First let the arrow of Thy piercing eye,
   Whose light outvieth the star-spangled skie,

Strike through the darknesse of my mind,
And leave no cloudy mist behind;
Let Thy resplendent rayes of knowledge dart   15
Bright beames of understanding to mine heart,
  To my sinne-shadowed heart; wherein
  Black ignorance did first begin
To blurre Thy beauteous image, and deface
The glory of Thy self-sufficing grace.   20

3. Next let the shaft of Thy sharp-pointed pow'r,
Dischargèd by that strength that can devour
  All difficulties, and encline
  Stout opposition to resigne
Its steely stubbornesse, subdue my will,   25
Make it hereafter ready to fulfill
  Thy royall law of righteousnesse
  As gladly as I must confesse
It hath fulfillèd heretofore th' unjust,
Prophane, and cruell lawes of its owne lust.   30

4. Then let that love of Thine, which made Thee leave
The bosome of Thy Father, and bereave
  Thyself of Thy trancendent glory,—
  Matter for an eternall story,—
Strike through mine affections all together;   35
And let that sun-shine cleer the cloudy weather,
  Wherein they wander without guide
  Or order, as the wind and tide

Of floting vanities transport and tosse them,
Till self-begotten troubles curbe and crosse them. 40

5. Lord, empty all Thy quivers ; let there be
   No corner of my spacious heart left free,
       Till all be but one wound, wherein
       No subtile sight-abhorring sinne
   May lurk in secret unespi'd by me,   45
   Or reigne in power unsubdu'd by Thee ;
       Perfect Thy purchas'd victory,
       That Thou maist ride triumphantly,
   And, leading captive all captivity,
   Maist put an end to enmity in me.   50

6. Then, blessed Archer, in requitall, I
   To shoote Thine arrowes back again will try ;
       By pray'rs and praises, sighs and sobs,
       By vowes and teares, by groans and throbs,
   I'll see if I can pierce and wound Thine heart,   55
   And vanquish Thee againe by Thine own art ;
       Or, that we may at once provide
       For all mishaps that may betide,
   Shoot Thou Thyself, Thou polisht shaft, to me,
   And I will shoot my broken heart to Thee.   60

34. THE INHABITING OF THE HEART.

God hath sent forth the Spirit of His Son into your hearts. Gal. iv. 6.

EPIGR. XXXIV.

Mine heart's an house, my Light; and Thou canst
tell
There's roome enough. O, let Thy Spirit dwell
For ever there, that so Thou maist love me,
And, being lov'd, I may againe love Thee.

ODE XXXIV.

1.   Welcome, great Guest; this house, mine heart,
          Shall all be Thine :
          I will resigne
Mine interest in ev'ry part ;
Only be pleas'd to use it as Thine own   5
For ever, and inhabite it alone :
There's roome enough ; and if the furniture
Were answerably fitted, I am sure
      Thou wouldst be well content to stay,
          And by Thy light   10
          Possesse my sight
With sense of an eternall day.

2.   It is Thy building, Lord ; 'twas made
          At Thy command,
          And still doth stand   15
Upheld and shelter'd by the shade

Of Thy protecting Providence : though such
As is decaièd and impairèd much
Since the removall of Thy residence,
When with Thy grace glory departed hence,   20
    It hath been all this while an inne
          To intertaine
          The vile and vaine
    And wicked companies of sinne.

3.   Although't be but an house of clay   25
          Fram'd out of dust,
          And such as must
Dissolvèd be, yet it was gay
And glorious indeed, when ev'ry place
Was furnishèd and fitted with Thy grace ;   30
When in the presence-chamber of my mind
The bright sun-beames of perfect knowledge shin'd ;
    When my will was Thy bed-chamber,
          And ev'ry pow'r
          A stately tow'r   35
Sweetned with Thy Spirit's amber.[73]

4.   But whilst Thou dost Thyself absent,
          It is not grown
          Noysome alone,
    But all to pieces torn and rent ;   40
The windowes all are stopt or broken so
That no light, without wind, can thorow goe ;

The roofe's uncover'd and the wall's decai'd,
The door's flung off the hooks, the floor's unlai'd ;
    Yea, the foundation rotten is ;   45
        And every where
        It doth appeare
    All that remaines is farre amisse.

5.   But if Thou wilt returne againe
        And dwell in me,   50
        Lord, Thou shalt see
    What care I'll take to intertaine
Thee ; though not like Thyself, yet in such sort
As Thou wilt like, and I shall thank Thee for 't.
Lord, let Thy blessed Spirit keep possession,   55
And all things will be well; at least, confession
    Shall tell Thee what's amisse in me,
        And then Thou shalt
        Or mend the fault,
    Or take the blame of all on Thee.   60

35. THE ENLARGING OF THE HEART.

I will runne the way of Thy commandments, when Thou shalt enlarge my heart. Psalm cxix. 32.

EPIGR. XXXV.

How pleasant is that now which heretofore
Mine heart held bitter—sacred learning's lore !
Enlargèd hearts enter with greatest ease
The straitest paths, and runne the narrowest wayes.

Ode XXXV.

1.   What a blessed change I find
        Since I intertain'd this Guest!
    Now methinks another mind
        Moves and rules within my brest.
           Surely I am not the same   5
           That I was before He came;
           But I then was much to blame.

2.   When before my God commanded
        Anything He would have done,
    I was close and gripple-handed,[74]   10
        Made an end ere I begunne;
           If He thought it fit to lay
           Judgements on me, I could say,
           'They are good,'—but shrinke away.

3.   All the wayes of righteousnesse   15
        I did think were full of trouble;
    I complain'd of tediousnesse,
        And each duty seemèd double:
           Whilst I serv'd Him but of feare,
           Ev'ry minute did appeare   20
           Longer farre then a whole yeare.

4.   Strictnesse in religion seem'd
        Like a pinèd pinion'd thing;
    Bolts and fetters I esteem'd
        More beseeming for a king,   25

Then for me to bow my neck,
And be at another's beck
When I felt my conscience check.[75]

5. But the case is alter'd now;
   He no sooner turnes His eye,   30
But I quickly bend and bow,
   Ready at His feet to lie;
      Love hath taught me to obey
      All His precepts, and to say,
      'Not to-morrow, but to-day.'   35

6. What He wills, I say, 'I must;'
   What I must, I say, 'I will;'
He commanding, it is just,
   What He would, I should fulfil;
      Whilst He biddeth, I beleeve;   40
      What He calls for, He will give;
      To obey Him is—to live.

7. His commandments grievous are not
   Longer then men think them so;
Though He send me forth, I care not,   45
   Whilst He gives me strength to goe.
      When or whither, all is one;
      On His bus'nesse, not mine owne,
      I shall never goe alone.

8. If I be compleat in Him,—   50
   And in Him all fulnesse dwelleth,—

I am sure aloft to swim
Whilst that ocean overswelleth;
Having Him that's All in All,
I am confident I shall
Nothing want for which I call.

36. THE INFLAMING OF THE HEART.

My heart was hot within me; while I was musing the fire burned.
Psalm xxxix. 3.

EPIGR. XXXVI.

Spare not, my Love, to kindle and enflame
Mine heart within throughout, untill the same
Breake forth and burne; that so Thy salamander—
Mine heart—may never from Thy fornace wander.

ODE XXXVI.

1. Welcome, holy heavenly fire,
        Kindled by immortall Love;
    Which, descending from above,
Makes all earthly thoughts retire,
        And give place
        To that grace
Which with gentle violence
        Conquers all corrupt affections,
        Rebell nature's insurrections,
Bidding them be packing hence.

2. Lord, Thy fire doth heat within,
    Warmeth not without alone:

Though it be an heart of stone,
Of itself congeal'd in sinne,
      Hard as steel,   15
      If it feel
Thy dissolving pow'r, it groweth
    Soft as waxe ; and quickly takes
    Any print Thy Spirit makes,
Paying[76] what Thou saist it oweth.   20

3. Of itself mine heart is dark ;
    But Thy fire, by shining bright,
    Fills it full of saving light :
Though 't be but a little spark
      Lent by Thee,   25
      I shall see
More by it then all the light
    Which in fullest measures streames
    From corrupted Nature's beames
Can discover to my sight.   30

4. Though mine heart be ice and snow
    To the things which Thou hast chosen,
    All benum'd with cold and frozen,
Yet Thy fire will make it glow :
      Though it burnes   35
      When it turnes
Tow'rds the things which Thou dost hate,
    Yet Thy blessed warmth no doubt

Will that wild-fire soone draw out,
And the heat thereof abate.   40

5. Lord, Thy fire is active, using
   Alwayes either to ascend
   To its native heav'n, or lend
Heat to others; and diffusing
        Of its store,   45
        Gathers more,
Never ceasing till it make
   All things like itselfe, and longing
   To see others come with thronging
Of Thy goodnesse to partake.   50

6. Lord, then let Thy fire enflame
   My cold heart so thoroughly,
   That the heat may never die,
But continue still the same ;
        That I may,   55
        Ev'ry day
More and more consuming sinne,
   Kindling others, and attending
   All occasions of ascending,
Heaven upon earth begin.   60

37. THE LADDER OF THE HEART.

In whose heart are the wayes of them. Psalm lxxxiv. 5.

EPIGR. XXXVII.

Wouldst thou, My love, a ladder have, whereby
Thou maist climbe heaven, to sit downe on high?
In thine owne heart, then, frame thee steps, and bend
Thy mind to muse how thou maist there ascend.

ODE XXXVII.

1. *The Soule.*

What !
Shall   I
Alwayes   lie
Grov'ling on earth,
Where there is no mirth?   5
Why should I not ascend,
And climbe up where I may mend
My meane estate of misery?
Happinesse I know's exceeding high;
Yet sure there is some remedy for that.   10

2. *Christ.*

True,
There is ;
Perfect blisse,
The fruit of love,
May be had above :   15

But he that will obtaine
Such a gold-exceeding gaine
Must never think to reach the same,
And scale heav'n's walls, untill he frame
A ladder in his heart as near, as new.   20

3. *The Soule.*

Lord,
I will ;
But the skill
Is not mine owne ;
Such an art's not knowne,   25
Unlesse Thou wilt it teach :
It is farre above the reach
Of mortall minds to understand ;
But if Thou wilt lend Thine helping hand,
I will endeavour to obey Thy word.   30

4-6. *Christ.*

Well,
Then, see
That thou be
As ready prest[77]
To performe the rest   35
As now to promise faire ;
And I'll teach thee how to reare
A scaling-ladder in thine heart
To mount heaven with ; no rules of art,
But I alone, can the composure[78] tell.   40

First,
Thou must
Take on trust
All that I say;
Reason must not sway   45
Thy judgement crosse to Mine,
But her scepter quite resigne;
Faith must be both thy ladder sides,
Which will stay thy steps whate'er betides,
And satisfie thine hunger and thy thirst.   50

Then
The round
Next the ground,
Which I must see,
Is humilitie;   55
From which thou must ascend,
And with perseverance end;
Vertue to verture, grace to grace,
Must each orderly succeed in 'ts place,
And when thou hast done all beginne againe. 60

38. THE FLYING OF THE HEART.

Who are these that fly as a cloud, and as the doves to their windowes?
Isaiah lx. 5.

EPIGR. XXXVIII.

Oh that mine heart had wings like to a dove,
That I might quickly hasten hence, and move
With speedy flight tow'rds the celestiall spheres,
As weary of this world, its faults and feares!

Ode XXXVIII.[79]

1. This way, though pleasant, yet methinks is long ;
   Step after step makes little haste,
   And I am not so strong
   As still to last
   Among   5
   So great,
   So many lets :
   Swelter'd and swill'd in sweat,
   My toyling soule both fumes and frets,
   As though she were inclin'd to a retreat.   10

2. Corruption clogs my feet like filthy clay,
   And I am ready still to slip ;
   Which makes me often stay
   When I should trip
   Away.   15
   My feares
   And faults are such
   As challenge all my teares
   So justly, that it were not much
   If I in weeping should spend all my yeares.   20

3. This makes me weary of the world below,
   And greedy of a place above,
   On which I may bestow
   My choisest love ;
   And so   25

Obtaine
That favour which
Excells all worldly gaine,
And maketh the possessour rich
In happinesse of a transcendent straine.   30

4. What! must I still be rooted here below,
    And riveted unto the ground,
        Wherein mine haste to grow
        Will be, though sound,
            But slow?   35
            I know
        The sunne exhales[80]
    Grosse vapours from below,
    Which, scorning as it were the vales,
On mountaine-topping clouds themselves bestow. 40

5. But my fault-frozen heart is slow to move;
    Makes poore proceedings at the best,
        As though it did not love
        Nor long for rest
            Above.   45
            Mine eyes
        Can upward looke,
    As though they did despise
    All things on earth, and could not brooke
Their presence; but mine heart is slow to rise. 50

P

6. Oh that it were once wingèd like the dove,
  That in a moment mounts on high !
    Then should it soone remove,
      Where it may ly
        In love :   55
      And loe,
    This one desire
  Methinks hath imp'd it so,
That it already flies like fire,
And ev'n my verses into wings doe grow.   60

39. THE UNION OF THE HEART.
I will give them one heart. Ezek. xi. 19.

Epigr. XXXIX.

Like-minded minds, hearts alike heartily
Affected, will together live and die;
Many things meete and part, but Love's great cable
Tying two hearts makes them inseparable.

Ode XXXIX.

1. *The Soule.*

All this is not enough ; methinks I grow
More greedy by fruition ; what I get
    Serves but to set
   An edge upon mine appetite,
   And all Thy gifts doe but invite   5
    My pray'rs for more.
Lord, if Thou wilt not still encrease my store,
Why didst Thou anything at all bestow ?

2. *Christ.*

And is 't the fruit of having still to crave?
Then let thine heart united be to Mine,   10
     And Mine to thine,
     In a firme union, whereby
    We may no more be, thou and I,
     Or I and thou,
But both the same; and then I will avow   15
Thou canst not want what thou dost wish to have. =lack

3. *The Soule.*

True, Lord, for Thou art All in All to me;
But how to get my stubborne heart to twine
     And close with Thine,
    I doe not know; nor can I guesse   20
    How I should ever learne, unlesse
     Thou wilt direct
The course that I must take to that effect :
'Tis Thou, not I, must knit mine heart to Thee.

4-7. *Christ.*

'Tis true, and so I will; but yet thou must   25
Doe something tow'rds it too. First, thou must lay
     All sinne away;
    And separate from that which would
    Our meeting intercept, and hold
     Us distant still :   30
I am all goodnesse, and can close with ill
No more then richest dïamonds with dust.

Then thou must not count any earthly thing,
However gay and gloriously set forth,
Of any worth,   35
Compar'd with Me, that am alone
Th' eternall, high, and Holy One:
But place thy love
Onely on Me and on the things above;
Which true content and endlesse comfort bring.   40

Love is the loadstone of the heart, the glew,
The cement, and the soder, which alone   = solder
Unites in one
Things that before were not the same,
But only like; imparts the name   45
And nature too
Of each to th' other; nothing can undoe
The knot that's knit by love, if it be true.

But if in deed and truth thou lovest Me,
And not in word alone, then I shall find   50
That thou dost mind
The things I mind, and regulate
All thine affections, love, and hate,
Delight, desire,
Feare, and the rest, by what I doe require;   55
And I in thee Myself shall alwayes see.

40. THE REST OF THE HEART.

Returne unto thy rest, O my soule. Psalm cxvi. 7.

EPIGR. XL.

My busie stirring heart, that seekes the best,
Can find no place on earth wherein to rest;
For God alone, the Author of its blisse,
Its only rest, its onely center is.

ODE XL.

1. Move me no more, mad world, it is in vaine;
   Experience tells me plaine
   I should deceivèd be,
If ever I againe should trust in thee :
   My weary heart hath ransackt all   5
   Thy treasuries, both great and small,
And thy large inventories beares in minde;
   Yet could it never finde
   One place wherein to rest,
Though it hath often trièd all the best.   10

2. Thy profits brought me losse instead of gaine,
   And all thy pleasures paine;
   Thine honours blurr'd my name
With the deep staines of self-confounding shame;
   Thy wisdome made me turne starke[81] fool,
   And all the learning that thy school   16
Afforded me was not enough to make
   Me know myself, and take

Care of my better part,
Which should have perishèd for all mine[82] heart.

3. Not that there is not place of rest in thee   21
       For others; but for me
       There is, there can be none;
That God that made mine heart is He alone
            That of Himself both can and will   25
            Give rest unto my thoughts, and fill
Them full of all content and quietnesse;
            That so I may possesse
            My soul in patience
Untill He find it time to call me hence.   30

4. On Thee, then, as a sure foundation,
            A trièd corner-stone,
            Lord, I will strive to raise
The tow'r of my salvation and Thy praise;
            In Thee, as in my center, shall   35
            The lines of all my longings fall;
To Thee, as to mine anchor, surely ti'd
            My ship shall safely ride;
            On Thee, as on my bed
Of soft repose, I'll rest my weary head.   40

5. Thou, Thou alone shalt be my whole desire;
            I'll nothing else require
            But Thee, or for Thy sake;
In Thee I'll sleepe secure, and when I wake,

Thy glorious Face shall satisfie   45
The longing of my looking eye ;
I'll roule myself on Thee as on my rock,
    And threatning dangers mock ;
    Of Thee, as of my treasure,
I'll boast, and bragge my comforts know no measure.

6. Lord, Thou shalt be mine All; I will not know 51
    A profit here below
    But what reflects on Thee ;
Thou shalt be all the pleasure I will see
    In anything the earth affords ;   55
    Mine heart shall owne no words
Of honour out of which I cannot raise
    The matter of Thy praise ;
    Nay, I will not be mine,
Unlesse Thou wilt vouchsafe to have me Thine. 60

41. THE BATHING OF THE HEART.

I will cleanse their bloud that I have not cleansed.   Joel iii. 21.

Epigr. XLI.

This bath thy Saviour swet with drops of bloud,
Sick heart, of purpose for to doe thee good.
They that have tri'd it can the vertue tell ;
Come then and use it, if thou wilt be well.

Ode XLI.

1. All this thy God hath done for thee ;
    And now, mine heart,

It is high time that thou shouldst be
　　Acting thy part,
And meditating on His blessed Passion,　　　5
Till thou hast made it thine by imitation.

2. That exercise will be the best
　　And surest meanes
To keepe thee evermore at rest,
　　And free from paines;　　　　　10
To suffer with thy Saviour is the way
To make thy present comforts last for aye.

3. Trace then the steps wherein He trode;
　　And first begin
To sweat with Him.　The heavy loade　　15
　　Which for thy sinne
He underwent squeez'd bloud out of His Face,
Which in great drops came trickling downe apace.

4. Oh let not then that precious bloud
　　Be spilt in vaine;　　　　　20
But gather ev'ry drop.　'Tis good
　　To purge the staine
Of guilt, that hath defil'd and overspred
Thee from the sole of th' foot to th' crown of th'
　　　　head.

5. Poison possesseth every veine;　　　26
　　The fountaine is
Corrupt, and all the streames uncleane;
　　All is amisse;

Thy bloud's impure; yea, thou thyself, mine heart,
In all thine inward pow'rs polluted art.   30

6. When thy first father first did ill,
      Man's doome was read—
That in the sweat of 's face he still
      Should eat his bread :
What the first Adam in the Garden caught,   35
The second Adam in a Garden taught.

7. Taught by His owne example how
      To sweat for sinne ;
Under the heavy weight to bow,
      And never linne   =cease 40
Begging release ; till with strong cries and teares
The soule be drain'd of all its faults and feares.

8. If sin's imputed guilt opprest
      Th' Almighty so,
That His sad soule could find no rest   45
      Under that woe,
But that the bitter agony He felt
Made His pure blood, if not to sweat, to melt,—

9. Then let that huge inherent masse
      Of sinne that lies   50
In heapes on thee, make thee surpasse
      In teares and cries ;
Striving with all thy strength, untill thou sweat
Such drops as His, though not as good, as great.

10. And if He thinke it fit to lay   55
        Upon thy back
    Or paines or duties, as He may,
        Untill it crack,
    Shrinke not away, but straine thine utmost force
    To beare them cheerfully without remorse.   60

42. THE BINDING OF THE HEART.

I drew them with cords of a man, with bands of love. Hosea xi. 4.

EPIGR. XLII.

My sinnes, I doe confesse, a cord were found
Heavy and hard by Thee, when Thou wast bound,
Great Lord of love, with them ; but Thou hast twin'd
Gentle love-cords my tender heart to bind.

ODE XLII.

1.   What ! could those hands
    That made the world be subject unto bands ?
            Could there a cord be found
    Wherewith Omnipotence itself was bound ?
    Wonder, mine heart, and stand amaz'd to see   5
            The Lord of liberty
    Led captive for thy sake and in thy stead ;
            Although He did
    Nothing deserving death or bands, yet He
    Was bound and put to death to set thee free.   10

2.   Thy sinnes had ti'd   [di'd ;
    Those bands for thee, wherein thou shouldst have

And thou didst daily knit
Knots upon knots, whereby thou mad'st them fit
Closer and faster to thy faulty self. 15
So, like a cursèd elfe,
Helplesse and hopelesse, friendlesse and forlorne,
The sinke of scorne
And kennell of contempt, thou shouldst have laine
Eternally enthrall'd to endlesse paine, 20

3.   Had not the Lord
Of love and life been pleasèd to afford
His helping hand of grace,
And freely put Himself into thy place.
So were thy bands transferr'd, but not unti'd, 25
Untill the time He di'd,
And by His death vanquisht and conquer'd all
That Adam's fall
Had made victorious : Sinne, Death, and Hell,
Thy fatall foes, under His footstool fell. 30

4.   Yet He meant not
That thou shouldst use the liberty He got
As it should like thee best ;
To wander as thou listest, or to rest
In soft repose, carelesse of His commands : 35
He that hath loos'd those bands
Whereby thou wast enslavèd to the foes,
Binds thee with those

Wherewith He bound Himself to doe thee good :
The bands of love, love writ in lines of blood.   40
[=bonds (ll. 36, 40)

5.   His love to thee
Made Him to lay aside His majesty,
          And, cloathèd in a vaile
Of fraile though faultlesse flesh, become thy baile.
But Love[83] requireth love ; and since thou art   45
          Lovèd by Him, thy part
It is to love Him too ; and love affords
          The strongest cords
That can be ; for it ties not hands alone,
But heads and hearts and soules, and all in one. 50

6.   Come, then, mine heart,
And freely follow the prevailing art
          Of thy Redeemer's love :
That strong magnetique tie hath pow'r to move
The steelyist[84] stubbornesse.   If thou but twine 55
          And twist His love with thine,
And by obedience labour to expresse
          Thy thankfulnesse,
It will be hard to say on whether side
The bands are surest, which is fastest tide.   tied 60

43. THE PROP OF THE HEART.

His heart is fixed, trusting in the Lord. His heart is established, he shall not be affraid. Psalm cii. 7, 8.

EPIGR. XLIII.

My weak and feeble heart a prop must use,
But pleasant fruits and flow'rs doth refuse;
My Christ my pillar is; on Him rely,
Repose, and rest myself alone will I.

ODE XLIII.

1. Suppose it true that, whilst thy Saviour's side
   Was furrowèd with scourges, He was ti'd
       Unto some pillar fast;
   Think not, mine heart, it was because He could
   Not stand alone, or that left loose He would   5
       Have shrunk away at last:
   Such weaknesse suits not with Omnipotence,
   Nor could man's malice match His patience.

2. But if so done, 'twas done to tutor thee,
   Whose frailty and impatience He doth see   10
       Such that thou hast nor strength
   Nor will, as of thyself, to undergo
   The least degree of duty or of woe;
       But wouldst be sure at length
   To flinch or faint, or not to stand at all,   15
   Or in the end more fearfully to fall.

3. Thy very frame and figure, broad above,
   Narrow beneath, apparently doth prove   =evidently
        Thou canst not stand alone
   Without a prop to boulster and to stay thee;   20
   To trust to thine own strength would soone betray
        Alas, thou now art growne   [thee.
   So weak and feeble, wav'ring and unstaid,
   Thou shrinkst at the least weight that's on thee laid.

4. The easiest commandments thou declinest,   25
   And at the lightest punishments thou whinest;
        Thy restlesse motions are
   Innumerable, like the troubled sea
   Whose waves are toss'd and tumbled ev'ry way;
        The hound-pursuèd hare   30
   Makes not so many doubles as thou dost,
   Till thy crosse courses in themselves are lost.

5. Get thee some stay that may support thee, then,
   And stablish thee, lest thou shouldst start againe.
        But where may it be found?   35
   Will pleasant fruites or flowers serve the turne?
   No, no; my tott'ring heart will overturne
        And lay them on the ground:
   Dainties may serve to minister delight,
   But strength is onely from the Lord of Might.   40

6. Betake thee to thy Christ, then, and repose
   Thyselfe in all extremities on those

His everlasting armes,
Wherewith He girds the heavens and upholds
The pillars of the earth, and safely folds   45
His faithfull flocke from harmes ;
Cleave close to Him by faith, and let the bands
Of love tie thee in thy Redeemer's hands.

7. Come life, come death, come devills, come what will,
Yet fast'ned so thou shalt stand stedfast still ;   50
And all the pow'rs of Hell
Shall not prevaile to shake thee with their shock,
So long as thou art founded on that Rock ;
No duty shall thee quell,
No danger shall disturbe thy quiet state,   55
Nor soule-perplexing feares thy mind amate.[85]

44. THE SCOURGING OF THE HEART.

A rod is for the backe of him that is void of understanding. Prov. x. 13.

EPIGR. XLIV.

When Thou withholdst Thy scourges, dearest Love,
My sluggish heart is slack and slow to move;
Oh let it not stand still, but lash it rather,
And drive it, though unwilling, to Thy Father.

ODE XLIV.

1. What doe those scourges on that sacred flesh,
Spotlesse and pure ?
Must He, that doth sin-weari'd soules refresh,
Himself endure

Such tearing tortures ?   Must those sides be gash'd,
          Those shoulders lash'd ?   6
Is this the trimming[86] that the world bestowes
Upon such robes of majestie as those ?

2. Is 't not enough to die, unlesse by paine
          Thou antidate   10
Thy death beforehand, Lord ?   What ! dost Thou
          To aggravate   [meane
The guilt of sinne ? or to enhance the price
          Thy sacrifice
Amounts to ?   Both are infinite, I know,   15
And can by no additions greater grow.

3. Yet dare I not imagine that in vaine
          Thou didst endure   [gaine
One stripe ; though not Thine owne thereby, my
          Thou didst procure ;   20
That when I shall be scourgèd for Thy sake,
          Thy stripes may make
Mine acceptable, that I may not grutch   = grudge
When I remember Thou hast borne as much,

4. As much and more, for me. Come, then, mine heart,
          And willingly   26
Submit thyselfe to suffer ; smile at smart,
          And death defie ;
Feare not to feel that hand correcting thee
          Which set thee free :   30

Stripes as the tokens of His love He leaves,
Who scourgeth ev'ry sonne whom He receives.

5. There's foolishnesse bound up within thee fast;
    But yet the rod
Of fatherly correction at the last,   35
    If blest by God,
Will drive it farre away; and wisdome give,
    That thou maist live,
Not to thyselfe, but Him that first was slaine,
And died for thee, and then rose againe.   40

6. Thou art not onely dull and slow of pace,
    But stubborne too,
And refractory; ready to outface
    Rather then doe
Thy duty; though thou knowst it must be so,   45
    Thou wilt not go
The way thou shouldst, till some affliction
First set thee right, then prick and spurre thee on.

7. Top-like[87] thy figure and condition is;
    Neither to stand   50
Nor stirre thyself alone, whilst thou dost misse
    An helping hand
To set thee up, and store of stripes bestow
    To make thee goe:
Begge, then, thy blessed Saviour to transferre   55
His scourges unto thee, to make thee stirre.

Q

45. THE HEDGING OF THE HEART.

I will hedge up thy way with thornes. Hosea ii. 6.

EPIGR. XLV.

He that of thornes would gather roses may
In his own heart, if handled the right way :
Hearts hedgèd with Christ's crowne of thornes, instead
Of thorny cares, will sweetest roses breed.

ODE XLV.

1. A crowne of thornes ! I thought so ; ten to one,
  A crowne without a thorne there's none ;
 There's none on earth, I meane ; what ! shall I then
  Rejoyce to see Him crown'd by men,
 By Whom kings rule and reigne ? Or shall I scorne
 And hate to see earth's curse, a thorne, 6
Prepost'rously preferr'd to crowne those browes
 From whence all blisse and glory flowes ?
  Or shall I both be glad,[88] ·
   And also sad,   10
 To thinke it is a crowne, and yet so bad ?

2. There's cause enough of both, I must confesse ;
  Yet what's that unto me, unlesse
 I take a course His crowne of thornes may be
  Made mine, transferr'd from Him to me ? 15
Crownes, had they been of starres, could adde no more
 Glory where there was all before ;
And thornes might scratch Him, could not make
  Him worse

Then He was made[89]—sinne and a curse :
    Come then, mine heart, take downe   20
        Thy Saviour's crowne
Of thornes, and see if thou canst make 't thine
        owne.

3. Remember first thy Saviour's head was crown'd
    By the same hands that did Him wound ;
They meant it not to honour, but to scorne Him,
    When in such sort they did bethorne Him. 26
Think earthly honours such,[90] if they redound
    Not to His glory, th' are not sound ;
Never beleeve they minde to dignifie
    Thee that thy Christ would crucifie ;   30
        Think ev'ry crowne of thorne,[91]
        Unlesse 't adorne
Thy Christ as well as him by whom 'tis worne.

4. Consider then, that as the thorny crowne
    Circled thy Saviour's head, thine owne   35
Continuall care to please Him, and provide
    For the advantage of His side,
Must fence thine actions and affections so,
    That they shall neither dare to goe
Out of that compasse, nor vouchsafe accesse   40
    To what might make that care go lesse ;
        Let no such thing draw nigh
        Which shall not spie
Thornes ready plac'd to prick it till it die.

5. Thus compass'd with thy Saviour's thorny crowne,
   Thou maist securely sit thee downe,   46
And hope that He Who made of water wine
   Will turne each thorne into[93] a vine ;
Where thou maist gather grapes, and to delight thee
   Roses, nor need the prickles fright thee :   50
Thy Saviour's sacred temples tooke away
   The curse that in their sharpnesse lay ;
      So thou maist crownèd be
      As well as He,
And at the last light in His light shalt see.   55

46. THE FASTENING OF THE HEART.

I will put My feare in their hearts, that they shall not depart from Me.
Jer. xxxii. 40.

Epigr. XLVI.

Thou, that wast nailèd to the crosse for me
Lest I should slip, and fall away from Thee,
Drive home Thine[94] holy feare into mine heart,
And clench it so that it may ne' er depart.

Ode XLVI.

1. What ! dost thou struggle to get loose againe ?
   Hast thou so soone forgot the former paine
   That thy licentious bondage unto sinne
   And lust-enlarged thraldome put thee in ?
   Hast thou a mind again to rove and ramble   5
   Rogue-like, a vagrant through the world, and scramble

For scraps and crusts of earth-bred base delights,
And change thy dayes of joy for tedious nights
    Of sad repentant sorrow ?
        What ! wilt thou borrow   10
That griefe to-day which thou must pay to-morrow?

2. No, self-deceiving heart, lest thou shouldst cast
    Thy cords away, and burst the bands at last
    Of thy Redeemer's tender love, I'll try
    What further fastnesse in His feare doth lie.   15
    The cords of love soakèd in lust may rot,
    And bands of bounty are too oft forgot;
    But holy filiale feare, like to a naile
    Fast'ned in a sure place, will never faile :
        This driven home will take   20
        Fast hold, and make
  Thee that thou darest not thy God forsake.

3. Remember how, besides thy Saviour's bands
    Wherewith they led Him bound, His holy hands
    And feet were piercèd ; how they nail'd Him fast
    Unto His bitter crosse ; and how at last   26
    His precious side was goarèd with a speare ;
    So hard sharp-pointed ir'n and steel did teare
    His tender flesh, that from those wounds might flow
    The sov'raigne salve for sin-procurèd woe.   30
        Then that thou maist not faile
        Of that availe,
Refuse not to be fast'ned with His naile.[95]

4. Love in an heart of flesh is apt to taint,
   Or be fly-blowne with folly; and its faint   35
   And feeble spirits, when it shewes most faire,
   Are often fed on by the empty aire
   Of popular applause, unlesse the salt
   Of holy feare in time prevent the fault;
   But season'd so, it will be kept for ever.   40
   He that doth feare because he loves will never
       Adventure to offend,
         But alwayes bend
   His best endeavours to content his friend.

5. Though perfect love cast out all servile feare,   45
   Because such feare hath torment, yet thy dear
   Redeemer meant not so to set thee free,
   That filiall feare and thou should strangers be;
   Though as a sonne thou honour Him thy Father,
   Yet as a Master thou maist feare Him rather.   50
   Feare's the soule's centinell, and keepes the heart
   Wherein love lodges so, that all the art
       And industry of those
         That are its foes
   Cannot betray it to its former woes.   55

47. THE NEW WINE OF THE HEART.

Wine that maketh glad the heart of man. Psalm civ. 15.

EPIGR. XLVII.

Christ the true Vine, Grape, Cluster, on the crosse
Trod the winepresse alone, unto the losse

Of bloud and life. Draw, thankfull heart, and spare not:
Here's wine enough for all, save those that care not.

ODE XLVII.

1. Leave not thy Saviour now, whatev'r thou dost,
    Doubtfull distrustfull heart;
Thy former paines and labours all are lost,
    If now thou shalt depart,
And faithlesly fall off at last from Him   5
Who to redeeme thee spar'd nor life nor limme.

2. Shall He, that is thy Cluster and thy Vine,
    Tread the winepresse alone,
Whilst thou standst looking on? Shall both the
    And worke be all His owne?   [wine
See how He bends, crusht with the straitned screw
Of that fierce wrath that to thy sinnes was due. 12

3. Although thou canst not helpe to beare it, yet
    Thrust thyselfe under too,
That thou maist feel some of the weight, and get
    Although not strength to doe,   16
Yet will to suffer something as He doth,
That the same stresse at once may squeeze you both.

4. Thy Saviour being press'd to death, there ran
    Out of His sacred wounds   20
That wine that maketh glad the heart of man,
    And all His foes confounds;

Yea, the full-flowing fountain's open still
For all grace-thirsting hearts to drinke their fill.

5. And not to drinke alone, to satiate   25
      Their longing appetites,
   Or drowne those cumbrous cares that would abate
      The edge of their delights;
   But when they toyle, and soile[96] themselves with
      sinne,
   Both to refresh, to purge, and cleanse them in. 30

6. Thy Saviour hath begun[97] this cup to thee,
      And thou must not refuse 't;
   Presse then thy sin-swoll'n sides, untill they be
      Empty, and fit to use 't;
   Doe not delay to come when He doth call,   35
   Nor feare to want where there's enough for all.

7. Thy bounteous Redeemer in His bloud
      Fills thee, not wine alone;
   But likewise gives His flesh to be thy food,
      Which thou maist make thine owne,   40
   And feede on Him, Who hath Himself revealed
   The bread of Life, by God the Father sealed.

8. Nay, He's not food alone, but physicke too,
      When ever thou art sick;
   And in thy weaknesse strength, that thou maist doe
      Thy duty, and not stick   46

At anything that He requires of thee,
How hard soever it may seeme to be.

9. Make all the haste then that thou canst to come,
    Before the day be past ;   50
And think not of returning to thy home
    Whilst yet the light doth last ;
The longer and the more thou drawst this wine,
Still thou shalt find it more and more divine.

10. Or if thy Saviour think it meet to throw   55
    Thee in the presse againe,
To suffer as He did, yet doe not grow
    Displeas̀d at thy paine ;
A summer season followes winter weather ;
Suff'ring, you shall be glorifi'd together.   60

The Spirit and the Bride say, 'Come.' And let him that heareth say,
'Come.' And let him that is athirst come. And whosoever will, let
him take the water of life freely. Revel. xxii. 17.   •

THE CONCLVSION.

Is this my period ?[98] Have I now no more
To doe hereafter? Shall my mind give o're
Its best imployment thus, and idle be,
Or busi'd otherwise? Should I not see
How to improve my thoughts more thriftily   5
Before I lay these Heart School-Lectures by?
Self-knowledge is an everlasting taske,
An endlesse worke, that doth not onely aske

A whole man for the time, but challengeth
To take up all his howers untill death.   10
Yet as in other schooles they have a care
To call for repetitions, and are
Busi'd as well in seeking to retaine
What they have learn'd already as to gaine
Further degrees of knowledge, and lay by   15
Invention whilst they practise memory;
So must I likewise take some time to view
What I have done, ere I proceed anew.
Perhaps I may have cause to interline,[99]
To alter, or to adde ; the worke is mine,   20
And I may manage it, as I see best,
With my great Master's leave.   Then here I rest
From taking out new lessons, till I see
How I retaine the old in memory.
And if it be His pleasure, I shall say   25
These lessons before others, that they may
Or learne them too, or only censure me ;
I'll wait with patience the successe to see.
And though I looke not to have leave to play—
For that this School allowes not—yet I may   30
Another time perhaps, if they approve
Of these, such as they are, and shew their love
        To the *School of the Heart* by calling for 't,
        Adde other lessons more of the like sort.

THE LEARNING OF THE HEART.

THE PREFACE.

I AM a scholar. The great Lord of love
And life my Tutor is; Who from above
All that lack learning to His school invites;
My heart's my prayer-book, in which He writes
Systemes of all the arts and faculties :   5
First reads to me, then makes me exercise,
But all in paradoxes, such high strains
As flow from none but love-inspirèd brains;
Yet bids me publish them abroad, and dare
T" excell[100] His arts above all other arts that are. 10
Why should I not? methinks it cannot be
But they should please others as well as me.
Come, then, joyn'd hands, and let our hearts embrace,
Whils't thus Love's labyrinth of arts we trace ;
I mean the Sciences[101] call'd liberal ;   15
Both Trivium and Quadrivium,[102] sev'n in all ;
    With the higher faculties—phylosophy,
    And law, and physick, and theologie.

THE GRAMMAR OF THE HEART.

That speaketh the truth in his heart. Psal. xv. 2.

My grammar I define to be an art
Which teacheth me to write and speak mine heart,
By which I learn that smooth-tongu'd flatt'ries are
False language, and in love irregular.
Amongst my letters, vow-wells I admit   5
Of none but consonant to sacred Writ;
And therefore when my soul in silence moans,
Half-vowel'd sighs and double deep-thong'd groans,
Mute looks and liquid teares instead of words,
Are of the language that mine heart affords.   10
And since true love abhors all variations,
My grammar hath no moods nor conjugations,
Tenses, nor persons, nor declensions,
Cases, nor genders, nor comparisons;
What-ere[103] my letters are, my word's but one,   15
And on the meaning of it love alone.
Concord is all my syntax; and agreement
Is in my grammar perfect regiment.
    He wants no language that hath learn'd to love;
    When tongues are still, hearts will be heard
            above.   20

THE RETHORICK OF THE HEART.

My heart is inditing a good matter. Psalm xlv. 1.

My rethorick is not so much an art
As an infusèd habit in mine heart,
Which a sweet secret elegance instills,
And all my speech with tropes and figures fills.
Love is the tongue's elixir, which doth change   5
The ordinary sense of words, and range
Them under other kinds ; dispose them so,
That to the height of eloquence they grow
Ev'n in their native plainness, and must be
So understood as liketh Love and me.   10
When I say Christ, I mean my Saviour ;
When His command'ment, my behaviour ;
For to that end it was He hither came,
And to this purpose 'tis I beare His name.
When I say, ' Hallow'd be Thy name,' He knows 15
I would be holy ; for His glory grows
Together with my good ; and He hath not
Given more honour then Himself hath got ;
So when I say, ' Lord, let Thy Kingdom come,'
He understands it I would be at home,   20
To raign with Him in glory : so grace brings
My love in me to be the King of Kings.
He teacheth me to say, ' Thy will be done,'
But meaneth He would have me do mine own,
By making me to will the same He doth,   25
And so to rule myself and serve Him both.

So when He saith, 'My son, give Me thine heart,'
I know His meaning is that I should part
With all I have for Him, give Him myself,
And to be rich in Him from worldly pelf.   30
When He says, 'Come to Me,' I know that He
Means I should wait His coming unto me,
Since 'tis His coming unto me that makes
Me come to Him ; my past He undertakes.
And when He says, 'Behold, I come,' I know   35
His purpose and intent is I should go,
With all the speed I can, to meet Him ; whence
His coming is attractive, draws me hence.
Thick-folded repetitions in love
Are no tautologies, but strongly move   40
And bind unto attention.   Exclamations
Are the heart's heaven-piercing exaltations.
Epiphonemæs and apostrophes
Love likes of well ; but no prosopepes ;
Not doubtful but careful deliberations   45
Love holds as grounds of strongest resolutions.
Thus Love and I a thousand ways can find
To speak and understand each other's mind,
And descant upon that which unto others
Is but plain-song, and all their musick smothers ; 50
    Nay that which worldly wit-worms call non-sence
    Is many times Love's purest eloquence.

THE LOGICK OF THE HEART.

Be ready always to give an answer to every man that asketh you a reason of the hope that is in you. 1 Peter iii. 15.

My logick is the faculty of faith,
Where all things are resolv'd into ' He saith ;'
And ergoes drawn from trust and confidence
Twist and tie truths with stronger consequence
Then either sense or reason ; for the heart   5
And not the head is fountain of this art.
And what the heart objects, none can resolve
But God Himself, till death the frame dissolve ;
Nay faith can after death dispute with dust,
And argue ashes into stronger trust,   10
And better hopes then brass and marble can
Be emblemes of unto the outward man.
All my invention is to find what terms
My Lord and I stand in ; how He confirms
His promises to me ; how I inherit   15
What He hath purchased for me by His merit.
My judgment is submission to His will,
And when He once hath spoken to be still.
My method's to be orderèd by Him ;
What He disposeth, that I think most trim.[104]   20
Love's arguments are all ' I will, ' Thou must ;'
What He says and commands are true and just.
   When to dispute and argue's out of season,
   Then to believe and to obey is reason.

Finis.

NOTES AND ILLUSTRATIONS.

[1] p. 107, '*Here's :*' spelled '*her's*' in first and second; '*Here's*' accepted from third edition.

[2] p. 107, '*at home.*' Cf. this and the whole poem with 'The Synagogue,' 50. Travells at Home. See our Memorial-Introduction.

[3] p. 107, '*sugard :*' a favourite contemporary word. 'Sugar' had still the romance of its distant source about it, and so was not *de trop.*

[4] p. 108, '*composure*'=composition. He means spirit added to body. Cf. HERBERT's 'Church Porch,' Glossarial Index, vol. ii. *s. v.*

[5] p. 109, cf. 'The Synagogue,' 42. A Paradox, last lines.

[6] p. 110, '*viprous brood :*' the allusion is to the belief that the birth of the viper's brood was the destruction of the parent. Cf. note in SOUTHWELL, &c. Milton works it into his conception of sin.

[7] p. 114, '*liest :*' printed '*list,*' which is misleading. So elsewhere in other like words, tacitly.

[8] p. 114, '*liver :*' supposed to be the seat of sensual or fleshly love. Cf. onwards.

[9] p. 114, '*frieth :*' see CRASHAW, Glossarial Index, *s. v.*

[10] p. 114, '*spumy*'=frothy.

[11] p. 115, '*behind :*' *i. e.* as a retributive Nemesis.

[12] p. 116, '*mind-amating*'=mind-subduing, mind-stupefying or foolish-making—the latter the usual sense, as used in English and Italian; the first the primary sense, as in mate at chess.

[13] p. 119, '*geason*'=what is rare, scarce, uncommon.

[14] p. 124, '*skinker*'=pourer out of liquor, tapster, butler, &c.

[15] p. 124, '*What it fills*' .... viz. man's dropsy, &c.; 'cormorant delight' may mean vast swelling, so as to fill with liquor or enormous thirst, thirst being often attendant on dropsy.

¹⁶ p. 124, '*welld:*' if=weld, *i. e.* unite, it is a curious use of the word : but query=wield or use ?

¹⁷ p. 125, '*idle complement:*' cf. HERBERT's Glossarial Index, vol. ii. *s. v.*

¹⁸ p. 125, '*market-place*'=common resort.

¹⁹ p. 126, '*beast:*' cf. HERBERT's 'Church Porch,' 6 ; Glossarial Index, vol. ii. *s. v.*

²⁰ p. 126, '*shelf*'=reef. Cf. HERBERT, ibid.

²¹ p. 128, '*Land-munger*'=dealer in or seeker after lands.

²² p. 128, '*livery and seisin:*' law terms=delivery and holding or possession (of land). See Glossarial Index to our Works of Sir JOHN DAVIES, vol. iii. *s. v.*

²³ p. 129, '*touch*'=tried by touchstone. See note ⁵⁶.

²⁴ p. 132, '*in grosse*'=in bulk. Cf. 'Synagogue,' 36. Trinity Sunday, l. 30, and relative note.

²⁵ p. 132, '*but*'=only, no otherwise than.

²⁶ p. 136, '*Cabinet:*' cf. p. 83, l. 19, and Glossarial Index to HERBERT, vol. ii. *s. v.*

²⁷ p. 136, '*All*'=universe, as in Donne, &c.

²⁸ p. 136, '*short-lin'd*' = whose natural circumference is measured by but a short line.

²⁹ p. 138, '*reprive:*' law term from French *reprehender*, to take back a sentence or prisoner : hence, secondarily, to stay what is going to be done.

³⁰ p. 139, '*antidate*'=make a hell on earth, despair being considered a chief torment of the damned.

³¹ p. 140, '*distresses:*' misprinted 'distresse' in first, second, and third. Cf. rhyme with 'premises.'

³² p. 141, '*thee:*' in first edition 'aile thee,' but in next line 'availe' only. Hence at first I felt disposed to read 'thee aile' and 'soon availe;' but I accept second edition.

³³ p. 141, '*reprieve:*' see note ²⁹.

³⁴ p. 142, '*parcell-devill:*' cf. Glossarial Index to HERBERT, vol. ii. *s. v.*

³⁵ p. 143, '*dresse*'== [for] thy God. So Shakespeare, 'look my twigs' ('All's Well,' iii. 6); and a similar omission of prepositions was not uncommon.

³⁶ p. 144, '*beck*'=nod : cf. p. 157, l. 40.

³⁷ p. 144, '*bared*'=which only when bared in submission and in Nazarite-like vow will be spared.

³⁸ p. 144, =and [then] brags that it attires [thee], though indeed it only cumbers thee.

[39] p. 145, '*writhen*'=made to writhe or twist.

[40] p. 146, '*calm'd and temperèd*:' imagery from the forge.

[41] p. 147, '*sheard*' = fragment of a potsherd : Job ii. 8, &c.

[42] p. 148, '*dole*'=give out, distribute.

[43] p. 149, '*mount*:' cf. ' The Synagogue,' 52. Engines, line 71, ' to mount a soul,' and relative note.

[44] p. 149, '*undeservèd praise* :' cf. Herbert in Memorial-Introduction to Harvey.

[45] p. 150, '*quest*.' Halliwell, as a North-country word, has this : ' Pies are said to be quested when their sides have been crushed by each other, or so joined to them as thence to be less baked.' He also gives qwaste as an old form of *quashed*, from Morte Arthure, Lincoln MS. Our word here is, perhaps, a form of *quash;* may be derived from Fr. *casser*, an early form of which was *quasser* (Cotgrave) ; Richardson, *s. v.*, gives *quassed* as an old form of *quashed*. The use of this provincialism, and of lay for lea=grass land, confirms Harvey's Cheshire or North-country birth. See Memorial-Introduction.

[46] p. 151, '*pearles* :' an old error that increased and grew from Pliny's time onwards. See Sir Thomas Browne's ' Vulgar Errors,' b. ii. 5.

[47] p. 151, ' *adamants*'=diamonds here.

[48] p. 153, ' *aqua regia* :' see ' The Synagogue,' 8. The Church, and relative note—a proof that ' Spirit's aqua regia' is the true reading.

[49] p. 153, ' *aqua fortis* :' a chemical allusion. Aqua fortis or nitric acid will not touch gold, but nitro-muriatic acid (aqua regia) does.

[50] p. 153, '*vaded* :' see an important note on this word *v.* faded in our edition of SOUTHWELL, Glossarial Index, *s. v.* ' *Di'd in graine* :' see note on this in ibid.

[51] p. 154, '*starke-wild* :' see notes [66] and [82].

[52] p. 159, ' *improve*'=daily bring about its virtues, as shown in stanza 5=bring them into play.

[53] p. 163, ' *tri'd* :' see note in our edition of SIDNEY, Glossarial Index, *s. v.*

[54] p. 164, '*sullen*'=(1) dark, as Shakespeare, ' bright metal on a *sullen* ground' (' 1 Henry IV.,' i. 2), and ' eyes fixed to the *sullen* earth' (ibid.) ; (2) *heavy, dull*, as Shakespeare, ' the *sullen* presage of your own decay' (' K. John,' i. 1).

[55] p. 164, ' *allayes*'=alloys : see HERBERT'S Glossarial Index, vol. ii. *s. v.*

⁵⁶ p. 165, '*touch*'=touch of trial as by touchstone. See note ²³.

⁵⁷ p. 167, '*misprision :*' technical legal term=contempt : next to capital offence.

⁵⁸ p. 168, =whilst the will pretends to have a privilege above the prerogative of reason—namely, that of making other things to move, while it is itself unmoved—rude passions leave serving the oar, to which, as slaves, they should be chained, to take upon them the guidance of the whole vessel of man.

⁵⁹ p. 168, '*bear thee in hand*'=delude thee—a common contemporary phrase=delude thee, that they &c.

⁶⁰ p. 168, '*prestigious*'=full of deceit : prestigate, to deceive as a juggler : Fr. prestidigitateur, Latin præstigiæ and -ator. The derivation unknown : perhaps from the frequent use of the word 'præsto' in jugglers' tricks.

⁶¹ p. 173, '*solid :*' cf. note in HERBERT, Glossarial Index, vol. ii. *s.v.*

⁶² p. 173, '*baites*'=bates : hawking technical term for attempting or preparing to fly at prey from the wrist or perch.

⁶³ p. 174, '*opacous*'=Latin *opacus*, impervious to light.

⁶⁴ p. 177, '*long remaine :*' having been lost with Ark at destruction of first temple.

⁶⁵ p. 179, '*lay :*' see note ⁴⁴.

⁶⁶ p. 180, '*starvy*'=cold and poor—a phrase still in common rustic use. It might have been '*starky*,' which is applied to land. Cf. starkish Line and starky West, Halliwell, *s.v.*

⁶⁷ p. 182, '*manure :*' cf. note in our SOUTHWELL, *s.v.* ; also Mr. Earle's note in 'Notes and Queries.'

⁶⁸ p. 185, '*then stone :*' I delete 'a' of first edition : in second edition it reads,

'By nature of itself more then a stone.'

The meaning of the latter is, 'no more moisture than a stone.'

⁶⁹ p. 186, '*Ocëan.*' So in 'The Synagogue.' See note ⁷³ below.

⁷⁰ p. 188, '*sun-observing :*' because it opens and shuts with the sun.

⁷¹ p. 188, '*orpin :*' a wound-herb.

⁷² p. 190, '*ramping :*' a heraldic term=rampant=rearing up as in attack.

⁷³ p. 193, '*admiration :*' 'tion' as dissyl. Cf. p. 186, 'Ocëan,' for like syllabic things.

[74] p. 198, '*amber*'=ambergris. See note in HERBERT, Glossarial Index, vol. ii. *s.v.*

[75] p. 200, '*gripple-handed :*' avaricious, griping, *i.e.* as to my efforts.

[76] p. 201, '*check.*' The meaning seems to be, I thought that if God would be obeyed as a King, it beseemed Him to put bounds originally to our will and our ways, rather than to give us a will to desire and do that which conscience (His law in us) denied and forbad.

[77] p. 203, '*paying :*' the previous line suggests the thought of coining; hence paying, &c.

[78 79] p. 206, '*ready-prest*' and '*composure :*' see Glossarial Index, *s.v.*

[80] p. 208, Ode xxxviii. Cf. for the form HERBERT's 'Easter Wings' and the Memorial-Introduction.

[81] p. 209, '*exhales*'=draws up. See Glossarial Index, *s v.*

[82] p. 213, '*starke :*' stiff, unbending; therefore that cannot be turned or bent to anything else, but is strongly itself. Hence stark-mad, &c. Perhaps more directly drawn from a corpse that is stark or stiff—a certain sign that the person is irretrievably dead, dead without hope of recovery.

[83] p. 214, '*mine :*' misprinted in all the editions 'thine.' It is=I should have lost my soul on account of my heart. See note on Ode xlv. st. 1.

[84] p. 220, '*Love :*' *i.e.* God (' God is love,' 1 John iv. 8).

[85] p. 220, '*steelyist :*' I change the spelling from 'steelist.'

[86] p. 223, '*amate :*' see Glossarial Index, *s.v.*

[87] p. 224, '*trimming :*' the red stripe of the scourging.

[88] p. 225, '*Top-like :*' cf. Ode xliii. 3.

[89] p. 226, '*glad :*' misprinted in all the editions 'clad.'

[90] p. 226, '*made—sinne :*' *i.e.* than He was made [being made] sin and a curse.

[91] p. 227, '*such*'=such [that] if.

[92] p. 227=think every crown to be one of thorn.

[93] p. 228, '*into :*' 2d and 3d editions misprint 'unto ;' and in line 49 'were' for 'where.'

[94] p. 228, '*Thine :*' 3d is 'Thy.'

[95] p. 229, '*naile :*' so in 2d and 3d editions, for 'nailes' of 1st edition.

[96] p. 232, '*soile :*' misprinted 'foile' in the three editions. 'Refresh' answers to 'toyle,' and ' purge and cleanse' to 'soile.' See note on Ode xl.

[97] p. 232, '*begun*'=first pledged or first drank the cup in health-giving. See note on 'begun,' in HERBERT, Glossarial Index, vol. ii. *s.v.*

[98] p. 233, '*period*'=end. Ibid.

[99] p. 234, '*interline*'=including both that follow, viz. to alter and to add.

[100] p. 235, '*excell*'=extol.

[101] p. 235, '*science :*' misprinted Sidemes.

[102] p. 235, '*Trivium and Quadrivium :*' Trivium, in the schools of the middle ages, was the name given to the first three liberal arts—grammar, rhetoric, and logic ; the other four —arithmetic, music, geometry, and astronomy—were named Quadrivium.

[103] p. 236, '*What-ere :*' 3d edition misprints 'what are.'

[104] p. 239, '*trim :*' see HERBERT, Glossarial Index, vol. ii. *s.v.*

G.

GLOSSARIAL INDEX.

As in the others, the most of the references give lesser or fuller explanations and illustrations of the several words. The various forms are placed under one word, as a rule.　　G.

A.
Account, 115.
Admire, 56, 59.
Adamants, 129, 151, 242.
Admiration, 193, 243.
Alchimy, 10, 90.
Alone, 12, 73, 91, 96.
All, 136, 241.
Allayes, 164, 242.
Amuse, 45, 93.
Amate, amating, 116, 223, 240, 244.
Amber, 198, 244.
Antidate, antidated, 15, 43, 44, 48, 139, 241.
Ape, 82.
Apparently, 25, 222.
Aqua-fortis, 153, 242.
Aqua-regia, 11, 153, 242.
Ascention, 54.
Attending, 38.
Attone, 39, 92.
Avail, 141.

B.
Ballances, 16.
Base-begot, 67.
Balsom, 77.
Bands, 127, 220.
Bared, 144, 241.
Baites, 173, 243.
Bell, bears the, 18, 91
Beck, 27, 144, 157, 241.
Beesome, 29, 92.

Bereaven, 55.
Beshrew, 62, 94-5.
Beautiful, seems, 70, 96.
Behind, 79, 115, 240.
Beast, 126, 241.
Begun, 232, 245.
Bear, thee in hand, 168, 243.
Bishop, 40.
Big-belly'd, 67.
Bitter-sweets. 77, 96.
Blazon, 44, 93.
Bloud, water, 49, 93.
Blabs, 69.
Blowes up, 149.
Bleer-ey'd, 174.
Bones, 12.
Book, by this, 20, 91.
Both, 226.
Braue, 60, 119.
Brine, 76.
Brags, 144.
But, we, but as, 49, 93, 132, 241.

C.
Carriages, 27.
Cards, 80, 96.
Cabinet, 83, 136, 241.
Calm'd, 146, 242.
Censures, 39, 92.
Chymick, 35, 92.
Check, 201, 244.
Circumcise, 49.
Circumvested, 87.
Close, 25, 91, 184.

8

Relent, 72.
Reprive, 138, 141, 241.
Riev'd, 51.
Riv'led, 122.
Rich-appearing, 128.

S.

Salvation, 42.
Sanctifi'd, 31, 92.
Sauc'd, xxiv.
Sciences, 235, 245.
Score, 63, 67, 95.
Sev'rall, 41.
Sense-dissolved, 115.
Sense-besotted, 119.
Sense-led, 119.
Shine, 28, 46, 93.
Shamefastnesse, 187.
Short-liu'd, 136, 241.
Sheard, 147, 242.
Shaken, 56, 62, 94.
Shelf, 76, 96, 126, 241.
Sincerity, 10, 11.
Sin-soyl'd, 29.
Sin-wearied, 223.
Sin-seised, 54, 94.
Sin-shaken, 84.
Sin-incensed, 48.
Sin-procured, 229.
Sin-shadowed, 195.
Skinker, 124, 240.
Slabbers, 81, 97.
Sleight, 130.
Smells, 92.
Solid, 173, 243.
Solidate. 12, 90.
Soile, 232, 244.
Sorry, 66, 95.
Soder, 212.
Spirits, 11, 90.
Spumy, 114, 240.
Stuff, household, 14.
Steely, 164.
Steelyest, 220, 244.
Starvy, 180, 243.
Stone, 185, 243.
Stupendious, 82, 97.
Strout, 84.
Starke, 149, 154, 242, 244.
Sublimated, 43.

Such, 227, 244.
Sun-observing, 188, 243.
Sun-shaming, 193.
Subterliminare, 5, 90.
Sugar'd, 107, 240.
Sullen, 164, 242.
Swarves, 167.
Swelled, 208.
Swill'd, 208.
Swell, 110, 240.

T.

Tail, 9, 90.
Take't, 109.
Teem'd, 68, 134.
Tenancy, 70.
Tempered, 146, 242.
Thwart, 6, 25, 90.
That, so, 9, 25, 91, 140.
Thorow, 51, 52, 74. 122, 123.
Third (=thread), 68, 95-6.
Thrall, 78.
Thyself, 80.
Thine, 228, 244.
Thunder-threatnd, 144.
Thee, 141, 241.
Tincture, 10, 90.
Touch, touchstones, 16, 87, 129,
    165, 241, 244.
Top, 17, 91.
Top-like, 225, 244.
Toothsome, xxiii., 23, 91.
Too-too, 26.
Tour, 55, 94.
Trivium, 235, 245.
Trim, 239, 245.
Trimming, 224, 244.
Transcend, 59, 94.
Transmigration, 83.
Trine-une, 136.
Tri'd, 242.
Tuch, 24, 91.
Turnings, 81.
Tune, 30, 92.
Twine, 220.
Tympaniz'd, 142.

U.

Unhook'd, 9.
Uncapable, 52.

𝕱𝖎𝖓𝖎𝖘.

LONDON:

ROBSON AND SONS, PRINTERS, PANCRAS ROAD, N.W.

www.ingramcontent.com/pod-product-compliance
Lightning Source LLC
Chambersburg PA
CBHW060603030726
47498CB00005B/1522